Cross-Fire

Cliff Farrell

THORNDIKE
CHIVERS

This Large Print edition is published by Thorndike Press®, Waterville, Maine USA and by BBC Audiobooks, Ltd, Bath, England.

Published in 2003 in the U.S. by arrangement with Golden West Literary Agency.

Published in 2003 in the U.K. by arrangement with Golden West.

U.S. Hardcover 0-7862-5938-8 (Western)
U.K. Hardcover 0-7540-7751-9 (Chivers Large Print)
U.K. Softcover 0-7540-7752-7 (Camden Large Print)

The text of this Large Print edition is unabridged. Other aspects of the book may vary from the original edition.

Set in 16 pt. Plantin by Myrna S. Raven.

Printed in the United States on permanent paper.

British Library Cataloguing-in-Publication Data available

Library of Congress Cataloging-in-Publication Data

Farrell, Cliff.
    Cross-fire / by Cliff Farrell.
        p. cm.
    ISBN 0-7862-5938-8 (lg. print : hc : alk. paper)
    1. Generals — Fiction.   2. Revenge — Fiction.   3. Large type books.   I. Title.
PS3556.A766C76 2003
813'.54—dc22   2003059139

Cross-Fire

Chapter 1

A shabby meeting house at the fork of a backwoods road in the brush along the Tennessee River bore the Biblical name of Shiloh. For more than twenty-four hours, seventy thousand men in two armies had fought a savage battle for its possession.

The mud around Shiloh had changed from brown to red. The water in the creeks ran crimson. The bodies of dead soldiers littered the fields. More were falling, reaped by the scythe blade of musket balls, canister, and 12-pound shells.

Kirby McCabe did not know that the place was called Shiloh. To him it was a nightmare, terrible beyond imagination. He was a soldier in the ranks, promoted to corporal only a few hours earlier, taking over for a comrade who had been killed.

He stumbled along, a bayoneted rifle, empty now, in his hands. He crouched, flinching, as the blades of the harvester howled around him. They touched his uniform at times, screeching in his ear with the voice of a demon.

On either side his companions were

being killed. Frank Williams fell a pace ahead of him. He and Frank had gone to school together back in their peaceful little home town on the Muskingum River in Ohio. They had been inseparable friends.

He stepped over Frank's body and kept going.

Around him, those who were still alive, were cowering beneath the harvester, just as he cowered. Some were praying. At least their lips were moving. Maybe they were cursing. Cursing the man who had sent them into this.

They all kept looking back — back at the life they were leaving. Now and then one would pause as though to retreat. In his face was the question that tore at the minds of them all. Why must I die? *Why me?* I want to live! *Live!*

Kirby also paused and looked back. Then, like the others, he moved mechanically ahead, facing the storm. That was the order. Charge! Any man who faltered would be shot. By order of Colonel Logan.

Better to die like a man than that. Die for the glory of Horace Logan who, most likely, was crouching safe and deep in some revetment, out of reach of the demons.

The brush was thinning ahead. Every

step carried them closer to the Confederate line. Kirby looked around. Thirty of them had left the shelter of the swampy grove in which the survivors of their battered regiment were pinned down, out of ammunition.

They were thirty no longer. They had the evil luck to have been handy when the colonel had needed men for sacrifice. A diversion, Horace Logan had termed it. A strategic maneuver to give the majority a chance to escape from the trap into which he had led them.

Keep the damned Rebs busy while the others fled. Charge the Confederate line! That was Colonel Logan's order when he had picked these men from Company A for the slaughter.

Die you may, and die you will, if need be, Horace Logan had told the top sergeant he picked to lead the thirty. But above all, buy time for the three hundred men who were all that remained of his command.

And never, never let the Confederate batteries suspect the presence of the ditch, knee-deep in water, but still passable, that offered the regiment a path through thick brush back to the main Union line.

The ditch was not marked on any map

and Colonel Logan was sure the enemy had no knowledge of its presence. It evidently had been gouged out by some farmer in the distant past, in order to drain swamp water from his cotton acres.

Charge! Thirty bayonets against the whirlwind. Thirty men advancing into the teeth of the demon that flashed bright crimson through the fog of powdersmoke. Backing the Confederate infantry were the batteries where at close range the gunners were double-shotting their pieces, using ninety-six balls of canister instead of the normal forty-eight. Brush around Kirby McCabe was being mowed by the reaper. Tall trees, their trunks rended, were toppling.

The top sergeant was dead now, lying somewhere in the red mud. Sergeant Jacobson was still alive and in command.

"Keep moving!" Jacobson kept screaming. "Charge!"

There was nothing else to do. There was no retreat unless a man preferred to be shot as a coward by his own comrades. Shot by order of Horace Logan.

Colonel Logan had his wish, at least. The Confederates must have believed a major attack was coming. The entire gray line was ablaze with gunfire that concentrated on the dwindling band of living dead.

"Keep moving!" Jacobson repeated. In the next instant, Sergeant Jacobson was dead, his life torn away by a cannon ball.

Kirby McCabe was their leader now. The corporal's mark, smeared on his sleeve with paint, made him that.

In command of what? He emerged from the brush into the open. With him were a handful of soldiers in blue. Half a dozen. That was all. One or two were staggering. Wounded. The others had fallen. He walked with ghosts. Ghosts of the comrades he had come to know as brothers during these weeks of war. Weeks? Or was it years since they had been given uniforms, drilled for a few days on the public square at Lockport, thrown in with thousands in camp, then marched into battle?

Half a dozen hollow-eyed youths, facing the sheet lightning of doom, confronted by the wrath of the world. Now there were five. Then four. Then two.

Then none as the bolts of lightning flashed and flashed and flashed again.

Kirby felt the bolt that struck him down. He was the last of the thirty to fall. It came almost as a benediction, erasing the sight of carnage, hiding the blasts from the furnace mouths of the cannon and the red serpent tongues of the muskets that sought his heart.

He had seen the others fall. He knew them all. Boys of company A. Goodbye to the flower of Lockport, Ohio.

He had only one other thought as the blackness gave him peace. He pictured himself clamping his fingers around Horace Logan's throat and never letting go. For Horace Logan had sent them to their deaths.

His next blurred memory was of voices, close at hand, mingling with the roar of baffle, muted now. "Heah's a Yank thet's still a-breathin', Cap'n. He's 'bout done fer anyway. I'd purely take pleasure in —"

"Never mind that, private," a stern Southern voice spoke. "You're too anxious to use that bayonet."

"He's nothin' but a damned shadbelly, Cap'n. Like the kind that killed my brotha yisterday. Maybe he done it, hisself."

The stern voice said, "Don't use that bayonet, I say. Maybe he can help us, if he lives long enough. Maybe he'll tell us how many more of his kind are down there in that patch of timber. And how we can get at them."

Pain again engulfed Kirby. The voices

and the drumfire of battle faded.

When he aroused, he found himself lying on straw in the open air. It was a field hospital that reeked of the misery and wreckage of the fighting. A harassed, stained medical man was bending over him with surgical tools in his hands.

The roar of cannon filled the world. Batteries, not far away, were firing as fast as powder and shot could be loaded.

"What's happening out there?" he mumbled.

The doctor said impatiently, "Lie quiet, Yankee. I've got to take your leg. You've been bad hit by canister."

Kirby, galvanized, pushed away the terrible instruments. "I'll kill you if you cut off my leg!" he gasped. "Let me die!"

"Have it your way," the medic said indifferently. "There're better men needing me."

Kirby realized that this was a Confederate field hospital, and he was their enemy. A prisoner.

He had a memory of having been babbling wildly, of men asking questions he did not want to answer. "I've been talking," he gasped. "They tried to pump me. What did I say? What did I tell them?"

Something like pity showed in the surgeon's weary eyes. "People say things when they're not in their right minds that they can't be held to blame for," he said.

The blackness descended again on Kirby. It lasted a long time. A full day. When he came back to awareness, he was on a steamboat, crowded with wounded soldiers. An orderly finally came to him. The orderly wore a blue uniform. A Union soldier.

"You was lucky, Corporal," the man told him. "You was captured by the Johnny Rebs, but we got you back when General Grant ordered a counter charge."

He added, "You're on your way to a hospital at St. Louis. The war's over for you."

Kirby lifted his head. He was almost afraid to look. But he still had both his legs, although one was encased in stained bandages.

He was not yet twenty years old on that day.

Chapter 2

He was twenty-four the August day he returned home. He had toughened, filled out across the shoulders. His skin was burned an Indian brown, making his hazel eyes seem pale. Tall, lank-legged, he carried himself with the straightness of one who had been astride a horse the greater part of the time.

Fine lines were beginning to web the corners of his mouth and eyes. A scar showed along the line of his left jawbone. That was where a Comanche buffalo lance had grazed him. He carried a fragment from a Kiowa arrowhead somewhere in his shoulder, and it sometimes gave him pain.

He stepped from the coach of a Baltimore & Ohio train that had brought him from St. Louis and stood on the old familiar wooden platform at the depot.

Home! The heaven he had longed for all these years of war. The beautiful dream that had kept fading away when he reached out to try to touch its substance. Now it was in his grasp.

He gazed around, avidly seeking the full zest of this moment, the glory of it. In his heart, fanfares were sounding. Flags were flying and bands were striking up in brassy triumph. Kirby McCabe was home! Home from the battles!

Around him, the scatter of other passengers who had alighted, faded off the sunblistered platform, heading for horse-drawn cabs, or for the shady side of Market Street, carrying their carpetbags and bundles. The faces of several of them had been familiar. He had known nearly everyone in Lockport by sight, if not by name.

But, if they gave him a second glance, it was to frown in instinctive antagonism. He was unforgivably different in manner and dress. No man in these parts carried a neckerchief slung around his throat. Or wore boots that had an alien cut to them. Spanish-made, they were, those boots, and they bore the scars of having carried heavy spurs. His hat had a brim far wider than was the custom, and its peak was taller. By glory, it had Spanish flavor to it also.

However, his breeches were federal issue. Lockport had seen many like them, worn by men who had come home after Appomattox. This familiar note proved that he had soldiered, but in all else he was alien. Lockport was always uneasy and suspicious in the presence of novelty or change.

Appomattox was more than a year in the past. The war was already becoming a memory. Ghosts like this sun-darkened, tall man had no part in Lockport's placid way of life. The war itself had been foreign too, like Kirby McCabe's garb. No thunder of cannon had ever reached this town. True, some of its wreckage had been cast up on Lockport's shores. Men had come home with arms or legs missing.

Few of Company A had ever returned at all. Those who had come back found that people weren't interested in stories of the deadly drabness of war. What they wanted to hear was the wild adventure of it. Those who had been there — at Shiloh and Chancellorsville, at Gettysburg or in the Wilderness — had little to say that they wanted to hear.

The sun burned down on Kirby as he stood gazing at his home town. Market Street had not changed. The hammer on the anvil in Jim Ransom's blacksmith shop still sounded its musical note. Al Roth's Inn had its customary line of idlers in the lobby chairs. It was market day, and women with baskets shopped in the square where the farmers had brought in their produce. Wagon and buggy horses switched flies at the tie rails along the un-paved street. The bell in the courthouse on Main Street boomed the hour. Ten o'clock. Ten o'clock on a peaceful summer day in a town that was changeless.

Only Kirby had changed. Sam Haskell, the station agent, came out of his ticket office, chalk in hand, to make a notation on the train board.

He halted, peering at the lone figure on the platform. "Say, ain't you George McCabe's boy?" he asked. "The one that went away to war with Company A?"

Kirby nodded. "Hello, Mr. Haskell. Yes, I'm George McCabe's son."

Sam Haskell's Adam's apple bobbed nervously. "You're the one that surren-dered to the Johnny Rebs at Shiloh, ain't you?" he asked.

Kirby stiffened. The fanfares began to fade. Sam Haskell's rheumy eyes seemed suddenly hard — and accusing.

"Surrendered?" Kirby said. "I'd hardly call it that." A pulse of anger began to throb in him.

Sam Haskell uttered a sniff and turned away. Kirby started to frame a question, then decided against it. He had carried off the train a possible bag which contained all his worldly possessions. He carried the bag

18

to the window of the baggage office. Sam Haskell, who was also the baggage agent, gave him a brass claim check without saying a word.

The possible bag was alien to Lockport also. It was made of buffalo leather, softened and tanned by Pawnee squaws on the Missouri River. Most folks carried their belongings in civilized satchels. Kirby's container was made to be thrown across a packsaddle or the back of a saddle-horse.

"So long, Mr. Haskell," Kirby said. When Haskell did not answer he headed up Market Street. He knew that Haskell was peering from the depot window, watching him.

He was alone. His mother had died when he was twelve, and he had learned that his father had passed away about the time of the Battle of Shiloh. There was an aunt and uncle or two and some cousins out in the farming country, but they had never been close, and did not count. Somehow, he sensed that they might not be happy to see him even if he did look them up.

The last of the bugles and the flutter of bunting had died in his heart. The day was marred. He became conscious only of the humid heat and the smell of dust

— and the indifference.

A block up Market Street a familiar face rose before him. Chuck Taylor. They had enlisted together, but Chuck had been with another regiment that day at Shiloh.

Kirby halted and said, a sudden thickness in his voice, "Hi-yuh, soldier. So you made it through?"

Chuck hadn't recognized him at first glance. Kirby guessed that he'd changed more than had Chuck.

Chuck instinctively thrust out his hand as the truth dawned. "Why, it's Kirby McCabe!" Then Chuck withdrew his hand. His manner changed. "So it's really you," he said distantly. "Yes, I made it all the way."

Here it was again. The strangeness. The covert doubt. The accusation.

Chuck added, "I see that you came through without damage too, from the looks. I heard you was taken by the Rebs."

"Not for long," Kirby said. "I —"

"We heard that too," Chuck said. "But some of the boys were held down there for a long time. Andersonville, Libby Prison. They had it mighty tough."

"I guess they figured I wasn't worth keeping," Kirby said. "They thought I was going to — to —"

His words faded. For Chuck had pushed past him and was continuing on his way down the street.

"To croak!" Kirby muttered, completing what he had started to say. But there was no one to listen.

He didn't understand. What was the matter with Chuck Taylor? And Sam Haskell?

He was puzzled. And suddenly afraid. He walked on up Market Street. He saw two or three more familiar faces, but their owners pretended they didn't see him.

Lockport's pride was the mansion of Horace Logan. It stood on high ground, overlooking the town and miles of the peaceful river. It had carriage houses and pergolas and limestone driveways winding among elms and buckeyes and maples.

It was a long, hot walk up hill to the mansion but Kirby was driven by a fierce urge. He had waited four years to meet face-to-face the man who had sent twenty-nine comrades to their deaths.

He walked up the flagstone path beneath the elms that tempered the heat of the sun. A colored gardener who was working in a plot of roses, paused, staring uncertainly.

A stableman emerged from the carriage house, wearing a gum apron and carrying

21

in his hand the sponge with which he had been washing some vehicle. This one started to approach, moving fast, intending to challenge Kirby's right to be there.

Something in Kirby's manner halted him. He remained at a distance, waiting. Kirby mounted the wide steps to the white-painted veranda, shaded by honeysuckle.

Somewhere in the big house someone was fingering out scales on a piano. The notes were sweet on the warm air. The front door was wide open for ventilation and he reached inside and twisted the key on the silver bell. The sound echoed in the house.

An elderly woman in a maid's cap and apron appeared on a circular stairway that mounted from the entry hall. Before she could descend, the piano playing ended and a young woman came hurrying from a side room into the hall.

She was young and shapely, with lively amber eyes and rich chestnut-hued hair that was held in a neat braid by an ornament. There was an assurance in her, the poise of one born to wealth and of a woman who knows the power of her beauty.

"What is it?" she demanded. Then she

looked him over a second time and he was sure there had been instant recognition — and apprehension in her.

Before he could answer, she added, "If it's work you're looking for, go to the carriage house and talk to Luke Stiles. He hires the stablemen."

She knew he wasn't here looking for work. It was her way of putting him in his place, of gaining the advantage. Attack was the best defense. Her father must have taught her that.

He knew who she was. As a boy he had watched many times from a distance as she rode by in a fine carriage with her parents or in a gleaming pony cart with a footman and maid watching over her. She was Horace Logan's daughter, Norah.

"I came to see Horace Logan," he said.

"*General* Logan," she said, "is not here."

General Logan! So he had come out of the war with stars on his shoulders.

"When will he be back?" Kirby asked.

"I would not really know," she said loftily.

"Where can I find him?"

Norah Logan suddenly became a little frightened of him. "I place you now," she said. "You're a Lockport boy who went to war with my father's regiment."

"I'm Kirby McCabe," he said. "Where can I find Horace Logan?"

His mention of his name had been no surprise to her. He was sure of that. She had known his identity the instant she had come to the door. She studied him, as though debating whether to answer or to close the door in his face.

In her was something of the curiosity and the accusation he had seen in Sam Haskell and Chuck Taylor. But there was also pity. This stirred anger in him once again. Pity from a Logan, of all people.

She decided to answer. "My father is out West. On business."

"Out West? Where out West?"

She met his brusqueness by trying to glare him into meekness. When that failed, she said stiffly, "In St. Louis." She smiled. "Not that it can be of any concern of yours."

"St. Louis?" The irony of it hit Kirby. "I have no luck. I was there only a few days ago."

"In St. Louis?" She was surprised. She gave him another suspicious appraisal. "My father is there with important men," she added, still trying to overawe him. "Senators and such. It's about the railroad. The railroad they're building to California.

24

If you were in St. Louis, then you know about it."

"I know about it," Kirby said. He could have told her that he even had a role in deciding the route the railroad was to follow over the Continental Divide. A minor role, but, nonetheless, a role.

The railroad they were building had been named the Union Pacific. Another company, called the Central Pacific, was said to he building eastward out of California with the idea of meeting the Union Pacific somewhere in the desert.

Kirby stood gazing at Norah Logan. He felt tired and cheated. He had lived over in anticipation a thousand times the moment when he would stand at the threshold of this house, call Horace Logan to his door and denounce him for the murder of those twenty-nine soldiers at Shiloh.

Perhaps even throttle him. Kirby had appointed himself judge and jury. And executioner, if need be. He felt that it would be keeping the faith with the others. With Frank Williams. With Sergeant Jakey. With all of them. It was a matter between only himself and the twenty-nine.

"So Horace Logan is in St. Louis," he said. "I'll go back there."

He started to turn away. A new voice

spoke. "Corporal!"

He halted. A man of about his own age had joined Norah Logan in the doorway. He was handsome and had the classic Logan features and the proud Logan mouth. He was Horace Logan's only son, Reid, and was a year or so older than his sister.

"Are you asking for a salute, Logan?" Kirby asked. "The war's over, or can't you reconcile yourself to forgetting that you were a lieutenant?"

"What do you want of my father, McCabe?" Reid Logan demanded.

"So you, too, remember my name?"

"I know you. Only too well."

"Strange," Kirby commented. "You never knew me when I was a tough kid, living in flatboat town along the river. Why is it that now you know me so well?"

"I'm sure you can answer that yourself, Corporal."

"The rank," Kirby said, "was captain when I was mustered out."

Reid Logan's brows lifted. "Well, well! Just what did you do to win your bars? The last we heard of you, you were in a hospital somewhere in Missouri, awaiting your discharge."

"They didn't discharge me. They wanted

to. I had a bad leg after Shiloh. I was no good to them as a foot soldier. But a man on a horse is the equal of anybody — if he wants to be. Have you ever heard of the 333rd United States Volunteer Cavalry? Some people called it the Border Cavalry?"

Reid Logan was silent for a space. The 333rd had fought a different type of war than the strife that had raged east of the Mississippi. With the withdrawal of troops from the frontier at the outbreak of the war, settlers on the plains had been at the mercy of the tribes who grasped the chance to clear their hunting grounds of the invaders.

To meet this threat, the Border Cavalry had been formed. It was composed of men, like Kirby, who had been wounded and were not available for infantry service immediately. Kirby, like his comrades, had preferred action to being assigned to some rear-line duty.

The Border Cavalry's war had been one of stealth and cunning, of surprise attack, of savage brutality and no quarter. The battlefield had extended down the Santa Fe Trail into New Mexico where the Comanche, Kiowa, and Apache were striking, and north to the great bend of the Missouri River in the Sioux country.

After a few months on the plains, Kirby's recovery from his wounds was complete. All that remained were the scars, and those on his mind were the deepest. He had found his proper place as a soldier. He became a plains cavalryman in the true sense of the word. He became not only a soldier, but a scout, a hunter, a superb horseman. A plainsman! Self-sufficient, tough of fiber and mind.

He and his comrades had been pledged to carry out the purpose of the regiment even at the cost of their lives. And give their lives they did. They died of starvation and fatigue. They died in blizzards and beneath the blazing sun of summer on the plains. They drowned in rivers and died at torture stakes in tribal villages. They died with arrows in their lungs and scalping knives slashing at them. Their graves were in bleak lands, and the fights in which they gave their lives would never find a place in history books. But they had died.

With them, the fighting had not ended with Appomattox. It had been more than a year since the peace on the Potomac had been signed before Kirby's company had been replaced and mustered out. On the day of his discharge he had worn the bars of a captain.

"So that's where you've been," Reid Logan said. "Well, fighting Indians was better than the Shenandoah Valley. Or Gettysburg, or the Wilderness."

"Have you even seen a woman impaled?" Kirby asked. "Or a baby's brains dashed out? Or a soldier who'd been tortured? There was no North or South out there. They were wives and children of soldiers on both sides. I'd hardly call fighting that kind of war a pleasure trip."

"There are worse things. Such as facing a firing squad. Or a hang rope."

Hang rope? Kirby had come here to denounce the Logans. Instead, he was finding himself on the defensive.

"I don't know what you're talking about," he said slowly. "But there are things even worse than that. Such as being the only one left alive out of thirty. Of seeing your friends killed."

Reid Logan was pale and grim. "Is that why you're here? You hold that against my father?"

"He's a butcher," Kirby said. "He tried to save his face by sacrificing thirty of us. He knew he was sending us to our deaths."

Reid Logan nodded. "He knew."

"Then you admit it?"

"It was his duty. If you were an officer, you know there are times when lives must be offered for the good of the majority."

"Sure. I know all about the responsibility of command. I've ordered men into places where they could be killed. And too many of them were killed. But I didn't *send* them in. I *led* them."

"My father had a regiment to save. What was left of it, at least. That was *his* responsibility."

"If he didn't have the sand to lead us, he could at least have sent some other officer. Our commander was a sergeant."

"I was the only other officer still on his feet at that time," Reid Logan said.

Kirby gazed at him ironically. "Well?"

"There's only one answer to that insinuation," Reid Logan said.

He was in his shirt sleeves on this humid day. He moved a stride forward and, with a flick of his left shoulder, struck Kirby in the face with the sleeve of his fine linen shirt.

The sleeve was empty! Reid Logan's left arm was missing!

In spite of himself Kirby felt a twinge of horror and pity. He looked at the empty sleeve. "I can't fight you, Logan," he said.

"You know that."

Norah Logan pushed between them. "Stop this! Stop it!"

Her brother moved her aside. "There's nothing wrong with my right arm, McCabe," he said. "I assure you I can shoot straight. Straight enough to kill you for that insult."

"No!" his sister cried. She again got between them. "The reason my brother wasn't sent with you that day was that he had been wounded. And he wasn't much more than a boy. He was only seventeen years old."

"There were others young enough to die that day," Kirby said harshly. "He was an officer. Old enough for that."

"A messenger boy," she sobbed. "My father's aide. And he had been wounded, I tell you. Who are you to accuse my father and my brother? You were the coward! The traitor!"

"Traitor?"

"You blame my father for the deaths of the men he sent out with you," she cried. "What about the three hundred who were slaughtered because of you?"

Kirby stared. "What are you saying?"

Reid Logan moved his empty sleeve. "This is one reason we remember you,

McCabe. You gave me this. I'll never forget you."

"I gave it to you? *Me?*"

"I was hit a second time that day. I left my arm in that ditch at Shiloh. When you brought the rebel batteries down on the regiment as we were trying to crawl out of that trap."

He refused to let Kirby speak. "Don't try to deny it! You were the only one who could have done it, McCabe. We know you were the only one alive. You were found in a rebel field hospital that Union soldiers overran the next morning in a counterattack. A Confederate doctor, who was captured, said that you had been raving, upbraiding your commander, who was my father. You said you'd hunt him down and kill him."

Kirby felt ice form inside him. He *did* remember saying things like that in his agony.

The two Logans were watching him. "You did it, didn't you?" Reid Logan said harshly. "You told them about that ditch. They shifted their cannon to enfilade it. They waited until they knew they had us dead to rights, then opened up. We were packed in like sheep. And slaughtered like sheep. Less than forty of us got back alive to our lines and the majority of us had been hit."

He waited for Kirby to speak, but Kirby was only staring at him, stunned.

"A rebel prisoner admitted to us afterward that their battery commander had been told about that ditch," Reid Logan went on. "There was only one answer."

Fury melted the coldness in Kirby. So that was why Sam Haskell had acted the way he did. And Chuck Taylor. That was why he'd been avoided as he walked the streets of his home town.

"It's a lie," he said hoarsely. "You know it's a lie! And so does Horace Logan!"

He wheeled and descended the steps. He almost broke into a run down the flagstone walk. He had come here to be the accuser and, instead, had found himself accused.

Norah Logan came racing with a swirl of her skirts and overtook him. She angrily seized his arm, halting him and forcing him to face her.

"What are you going to do?" she demanded.

When he didn't answer, she tried to shake him. "You came here to harm my father," she said huskily. "Kill him perhaps. Didn't you?"

Her strength was fierce, demanding.

"Answer me!" she insisted.

"Maybe," Kirby said. "Maybe I did."

"And you still intend to harm him?"

"I had heard that the rest of the regiment had been slaughtered in that ditch," he said slowly. "But I didn't know until this moment that Horace Logan had shouldered off the blame on me."

He added, "Nothing's changed. He can't escape responsibility. I'll find him."

Her hand dropped from his arm. His expression seemed to terrify her. He left her standing there and walked to the street and away from the mansion. Reid Logan still stood watching from the veranda, his empty sleeve swinging in the stir of the hot Ohio breeze.

Kirby returned to the depot and paid Sam Haskell a nickel for looking after his possible bag. He inspected the train board and saw that a westbound express was due soon.

He drew out his money poke and counted out some of the gold coins the government had paid him when he had been mustered out. He had let his pay accumulate during his years of service and was well fixed for funds.

"Where to?" Sam Haskell asked when he moved to the ticket cage.

"St. Louis," Kirby said.

"Do you reckon that's far enough?" Haskell commented, eying him insolently.

Kirby paid for the ticket and pocketed the change. He ran an arm suddenly through the window, caught Sam Haskell by the front of his shirt, shook him savagely, then tossed him back against the wall with a violence that jarred the man to his heels.

"Someday, I'll be back, you pup!" he said.

"I'll find Horace Logan," he added, "I'll find him and make him tell the truth."

Chapter 3

Horace Logan was not in St. Louis.

"Gineral Logan an' a passel of other big-wigs pulled out fer Omaha City nigh onto a week ago," Kirby's informant, who was first mate on a river packet, said. "They was wearin' silk hats an' reeked of money. The gineral an' his crowd has been buzzin' back an' forth betwixt here an' Omaha City for quite a spell, busier'n a bear at a honey tree. They say the gineral aims to git a big slice o' the railroad pie. Maybe take over the whole railroad. If you ask me, he's the man who can do it, too."

The pie, of course, was the Union Pacific Railroad. Kirby boarded the next steamboat, bound for Omaha on the Missouri River. Only deck room was to be had. He slept under a tarpaulin in a driving rain on the prow of a battered sidewheeler which still bore scars of Confederate shells. It carried a topheavy load of steel rails and passengers.

It was early dusk, two days later, when he stepped ashore. The rain had stopped and the weather had turned hot, but the

36

river was high and muddy, evidently from storms on the plains.

He stared. He had seen Omaha some two years in the past when he was with the Border Cavalry, en route to campaign against the Cheyennes. It had been a sleepy river settlement, huddling close to the high bank of the Missouri, awakening only to the whistles of approaching packets, bound for military forts upriver.

Now, Omaha was a noisy, human anthill. A score of steamboats were moored along the shore. Rafts of railroad ties that had been floated down from the Black Hills, or barged in from St. Louis, were penned in chain stocks downstream. Machine shops and warehouses flanked the town. A maze of railroad tracks was in operation. Steel had already advanced miles westward, but Omaha was still the base, the supply point, the pulsing heart of the operation. Everywhere, on shops, on locomotives, on cars, appeared the magic name that had brought this settlement to life.

Union Pacific!

Kirby made his way up the principal thoroughfare. Omaha had pretentious new buildings and hotels — and around them a conglomeration of jerry-built shacks and tents. There were a few stretches of brick and duckboard sidewalks, but mainly the restless streams of pedestrians walked in dust. Jerkline teams and spans of oxen strained in the unpaved streets to move wagons that were down to their hubs in the mud from the previous day's rains.

This was Boom Town. This Omaha was something new on the face of the prairie, amazing and unbelievable. He walked along the teeming street, delighted and fascinated. The hectic vitality, the rawness, the swaggering impudence of it caught him up and carried him along in its tide.

Westward lay blank spaces on the map. Why, there were buffalo out there in less than a day's ride. And likely Indians who would kill and scalp.

But here were men in frock coats and silk hats, and women in ribbons and stays and holding satin petticoats out of the mud as they were helped into fine carriages. Here was music and the blare of barkers at gambling traps and the fandango parlors. Bearded plainsmen in hide jackets, stained with the blood of buffalo and beaver, rubbed shoulders with Army officers in dress uniforms.

A man blocked Kirby's path. He veered and found the same impediment in his way. His annoyer was grinning.

Kirby halted and began laughing. "Why, you damned Alabama shoofly, get out of my way before I step on you and squash you."

Then they were shaking hands with the hard grip of men who had faced danger and privation together.

"What are you doing in this madhouse, Lee?" Kirby demanded.

"Dealin' a little faro now an' then," Lee Venters said. He spoke with the soft roll of the South in his voice. When he chose, he could thicken it to the dialect of an uneducated backwoods cracker. The fact was that he came from a prominent plantation family.

He had been a member of Jeb Stuart's Confederate raiders, but had been wounded and captured by Union troops early in the war. Because his wife and young daughter were in Denver, which was exposed to Indian raids, he had been paroled out of Union prison on condition that he join the Border Cavalry as a mule packer, a duty which would theoretically make him a noncombatant. He had, in fact, been a member of the 333rd's fighting squads when they were campaigning in the Dakota country against the Sioux. He and Kirby had become very close friends.

"It's been quite a spell since I've had the privilege of buyin' you a mild libation or two," Lee said. "Nigh onto a year, I reckon, since I was detached for duty down on the Arkansas River. I was mustered out three, four months ago. An' you?"

"About four weeks ago," Kirby said. "At Fort Leavenworth. I heard you got hit with a Kiowa musket slug somewhere down on the Picketwire. I guess a hide as tough as yours just naturally bounced it right back at them."

"It tickled a little," Lee admitted. "They sent me to Denver to recuperate. I had a mighty fine nurse there."

"Stella, of course, you lucky dog. So you finished out the war lying in bed, being spoon-fed by your beautiful wife. The rest of us poor devils stayed up on the plains, sleeping in buffalo wallows and freezing in blizzards. There weren't any pretty gals around up there, let me state emphatically. Nothing but some ugly squaws who had ambitions about skinning us alive."

Kirby added, "And how is Stella?"

"Fine! Fine! Gittin' purtier'n sassier every day. You'll see her directly. She's here with me in Omaha, o' course."

"And little Timmy? How is she?"

A twinkle came in Lee Venters' eyes. "*Little* Timmy's fine too. She's here with us."

"Great!" Kirby said. "Let's see, it must be more than two years since I last saw Stella and Timmy. That was back in Denver during that wonderful winter when we were garrisoned there for months. Timmy likely will soon be starting to grow up."

Lee grinned. "She'll be doin' that for sure."

He linked arms with Kirby. "Fall in an' I'll lead you to the only place in town where you'll drink good Tennessee mountain dew. It's furnished to me by an ol' friend o' mine I rode with under Jeb Stuart, an' who has now gone back to his old hobby at his still which he has set up either up or down the river, I don't recollect which."

They walked down the street and swung, arm-in-arm, through the swing doors of a gambling house whose sign proclaimed it as the FOUR ACES.

It was a sizable place, with a canvas roof and walls, half canvas, half wooden. Also a wooden floor, covered with sawdust. A bar stood to the left, extending part way down the room, but the principal business here was gambling. In addition to poker tables, roulette, a birdcage game and a faro bank were in operation. The tables were only sparsely patronized at this supper hour.

Kirby eyed his friend, his brows lifting.

Lee grinned. "Looks just as though it was still in Denver, don't it?" he said. "It's the same old Four Aces, but it's what you might call movable, now. We're equipped to knock it down in an hour's time, load it on a flatcar an' move west to end o' steel . . . which we'll be doin' in a few days. To a place called Nebraska City. Steel will be reachin' there most any day."

Lee Venters had always been a chance-taker, a gambler who loved to play for high stakes — such as riding with Jeb Stuart.

"See anyone you know?" he asked.

Kirby's gaze traveled around the room. He suddenly pushed back his hat, gave Lee a grinning look and walked to the bar where a man stood alone, drinking beer.

"Howdy, Ray," Kirby said.

Raymond Coleman turned. His eyes widened. "I can't believe it!" he exclaimed. "Kirby! Why, you rascal!"

Raymond Coleman was a wiry man in his middle forties with a grip like steel. He was tanned cinnamon-brown and had deep sun and weather wrinkles around his eyes and mouth. His sandy hair was thinning. He dressed conservatively, but allowed himself one ostentation in the shape of a long, sorrel-colored mustache which he kept carefully trimmed and waxed.

He and Kirby stood smiling, their hands clasped. It had been while Kirby was campaigning against the Comanches on the Santa Fe Trail that he had been detailed with a troop to guard a party of railroad surveyors that was mapping the country as far as the Continental Divide in Arizona Territory.

Raymond Coleman had been the leader of the mapping party. The Civil War had been raging, but the far-seeing Abraham Lincoln had insisted that preparations for a railroad to California must not be abandoned because of the conflict.

Kirby and Ray Coleman had soon become close friends. Kirby began helping with the surveying and mapping. He read books on engineering that the older man gave him.

The central route across the plains, which was the one generally followed by the Overland Stage, had been tentatively selected as the path for building a railroad to the Pacific Coast. However, it had been Coleman's task to survey every possible alternative before a final commitment was made.

It was a strenuous task that had kept Coleman busy for more than three years. He was an expert in his field — perhaps the best in the world, Kirby learned. And influential. Just how influential, Kirby discovered, when he found himself promoted to a lieutenancy by direct order from the White House, and given the responsibility of permanently commanding the detail that guarded Raymond Coleman's surveying parties.

He had virtually become Coleman's assistant, rather than a military aide. And Coleman's exhaustive report was responsible, as much as any other factor, in the final decision to build by the central route.

While Coleman had found that several other paths were feasible, he had recommended the central overland as the most economical at the moment.

Lee Venters had been with the detail during the dangerous months of surveying routes in the Dakota country, with the Sioux frowning on their efforts. The three of them stood looking at each other, remembering back.

They talked the same language, were comfortable in each other's company and respected their various prowess. Kirby, the youngest of the trio, had been the impetuous one. He had a head for the complicated mathematics with which Ray Coleman dealt, where Venters, the gambler, only played hunches. But both of them had sat at Coleman's knee when the final equations were made in which an error of judgment could cost millions to investors.

"This," said Ray Coleman, "is a reunion that calls for nothing less than champagne. Let us sit and talk about the good old days when we slept in the mud, drank gyp water from alkali pools and even a tough old sage hen tasted like fat bull."

"Champagne?" Kirby said incredulously. "Do you really mean there's bubble-water in this country now?"

"The better things of life are reaching Omaha," Coleman said. "And the worst."

The bottle that was brought was of good vintage. They clinked glasses. "To Dakota mud," Lee said.

They drank. "What brings you here, Kirby?" Coleman asked. "I hope it's a job you're hunting. In that case, remember that I'm the first to offer you one."

He lifted a hand to silence Kirby before an answer could be made. "I won't take no.

You've never seen the beautiful Spanish señoritas in California, my boy. You should pay me for giving you the opportunity. However, I'll be a squanderer and offer you money for the privilege. Two hundred and fifty a month."

"Two fifty?" Kirby exclaimed. "That's a fortune to what they paid me in the 333rd. And I had to buy my own boots. What do I do to earn this? Rob the poor and give it to the rich?"

"Men are building railroads these days, my friend. And they are in a hurry. They're laying steel, not only from this end, but from California. Across the Sierra Nevadas. Big tough mountains. Then the Ute Desert. I'm heading for Sacramento tomorrow."

"That soon?"

"Ted Judah, an old friend, did the preliminary locating for the Central Pacific, but Ted died a year or so ago. I've been asked by Collis Huntington and Leland Stanford, who are backing the C.P., to work for them. They aim to push their railroad east faster than the U.P. builds west."

He eyed Kirby. "I'll need men I know will hang tough with me. You couldn't have shown up at a better time."

Kirby shook his head. "I'd like to go. I've

46

never seen California. The money is more than good. But I can't."

Coleman was disappointed. "You've got something better in mind?"

"Maybe not better," Kirby said.

He turned to Lee Venters, changing the subject. "Owning the Aces is a mighty long yell from chasing Indians. You look slick and fat. You're still being spoon-fed, I take it."

"It's a livin'," Lee said. "Faro bankin' is about the only trade I know. You never get rich, dealin' a level game. An' here comes the one that sees it's on the level. My case keeper."

A woman had appeared in the gambling house. A stir of interest ran through the place. Eyes followed her. She was a mature, shapely person, with coppery golden hair and good gray eyes. She wore a modest dark dress that complemented her hair and figure. She nodded to players here and there, smiling. There was nothing brazen in her manner or garb.

She spotted Kirby and came hurrying, her eyes wide. "Kirby! Kirby McCabe! Where did you come from? Why didn't you let us know?" She kissed Kirby, shaking him with reproach.

"Stella, how do you do it?"

"Do what?"

47

"Keep growing prettier all the time."

She kissed her husband. "Listen to him, Lee, and take note. He still knows how to flatter the ladies. On second thought, I don't want you to learn."

"Kirby was asking about our little girl," Lee said, and again he was grinning. "Little Timmy. Just what was the situation with her tonight?"

Stella laughed. "Tragic. Utterly dismal. It was something about her hair as I was leaving. She was mentioning that she might enter a convent so she wouldn't have to face the world with such awful hair."

She smiled. "Timmy's at the frightful age of sixteen. A freckle is a cause for tears. Two freckles are a major calamity. Tonight, it's her hair. Hay-colored, she calls it. It's really honey blonde. She's very attractive."

"Did you say sixteen?" Kirby asked. "That's impossible, of course. That'd make you about ten when she was born."

"Thank you, dear. You fibber. I'm thirty-five and you know it."

"I'm afraid we've got to get to work," her husband said. "If you two will excuse us, we'll open the bank for an hour, an' then all go to supper. When Stella keeps cases for me, we always seem to have every chair filled. I don't understand it."

Stella laughed again. "I see that you *are* learning, darling. We'll dine at eight o'clock. Don't try to refuse, either of you. This is an occasion. A reunion. We have a housekeeper who can cook the most delicious meals. I'll send word to her to put her best foot forward. Timmy will be just delighted to see you, Kirby."

The Venters moved to where a floor man was removing the cover from the faro table. The chairs were already filling.

"Lee's a lucky man," Kirby said.

Ray Coleman nodded. "It's a hard life for both of them. But there's not much choice. The South is smashed flat. What Sherman didn't destroy, the carpetbaggers are stealing. There's a measure of vengeance in this for them. The money Lee wins is Northern money. I guess they both figure it's no sin to take it."

Darkness had come. The evening play was setting in. Action had picked up at the tables. The faro game the Venters operated was the center of attraction for bystanders.

Kirby noted the expressions on the faces of men as they watched Stella's slim fingers move the markers on the case. There was loneliness in many eyes, longing and envy in others.

"It's like it was in Denver," he commented to Coleman. "They used to ride days out of their way to look at her."

He ordered beer. He and Coleman sat exchanging reminiscences and news of men they had ridden with during the mapping trips.

Kirby finally brought up the subject uppermost in his mind but which he had been avoiding. "Speaking of railroads, I understand there's a covey of rich men who came here from St. Louis to get a finger in the financial pie in the U.P. I suppose you've met them."

Coleman did not respond for a moment and Kirby began to believe he had not been listening. Then Coleman spoke. "Horace Logan is here in Omaha. That's what you really wanted to know, isn't it?"

Kirby didn't answer. None was necessary. Raymond Coleman was the only person to whom he had told the story of Shiloh. He had related it to the older man one night in a lonely camp on the plains in the same way he would have talked to his father, if his father had been alive. Ray Coleman had listened in silence, knowing that it was something Kirby had to talk about to someone. It had been bottled up inside him too long.

"Don't, Kirby," Coleman now said

gently. "Don't let this thing fester inside you any longer. How long has it been? Four years. It was war. Part of the madness of it. There's never anything right in war. It's all wrong, all a nightmare."

"So he *is* here?" Kirby said.

"And so?"

Kirby's face was stony. "I promised some friends of mine that I'd make him answer."

"Friends?"

"The ones who are still at Shiloh. They can't face him themselves. Not on this earth."

Coleman sighed. "Come to California with me, Kirby. There's work to do there. Good, interesting work. Three or four years of it. Maybe more. There's nothing here in Omaha for you. Taking vengeance on Horace Logan won't bring back the others. It'll only ruin your own life."

"There's more to it, since I last saw you." Kirby said. "He's labeled me as a coward and a traitor. He's accusing me of causing the slaughter of the regiment."

He recounted what he had learned in Lockport. "People I'd known almost since I was born looked at me as though I was unclean," he said. "I came here to force the truth out of Horace Logan. Choke it out of him, if need be. Where can I find him,

51

Ray? You've seen him. Is he still here?"

Coleman debated for a long time whether to answer. He finally spoke reluctantly. "Yes, I've seen him. And within the last few hours, to tell the truth. I've never met the man personally, but know him by reputation, of course. A friend pointed him out to me on the street this afternoon. I understand he came here with intentions of trying to grab control of the Union Pacific, but was surrounded by some questionable characters. It was a game of wits between millionaires."

"Millionaires? Horace Logan is *that* rich now?"

"So I'm told. He was well off before the war and his investments did well while he was soldiering. He made big money in Eastern railroads. There's talk that he was threatening to form a syndicate and build another railroad to California unless he was allowed in on the ground floor in the Union Pacific."

"Even millionaires couldn't handle a job that big, could they?" Kirby asked. "The newspapers talk about the Union Pacific's financial troubles, even with the government backing it."

"It's far from impossible," Coleman said. "The U.P.'s troubles are mainly the work of greedy politicians. But there's a lot of idle money in the world. They know in Europe, and in England especially, that this Western country is ripe for development. And for making fortunes. Canada also. I was approached only a few days ago by a British syndicate. They were wondering if a railroad through the northern plains would be feasible."

"And would it?"

"Not at this moment, with the Union Pacific being built. Later, yes. And not a great while later. As you know, we surveyed one very adequate route from the Missouri into the Sioux country. North of Squaw Buttes and Squaw River. They're already building a railroad across the Iowa prairie to the upper Missouri River. When the time is ripe they'll continue building across the plains. The money can he raised. It's what they do with the money afterward that causes the trouble."

"Trouble?"

Coleman nodded toward a group of men who were entering the Four Aces. "That kind of trouble."

There were four of them. Two were well-dressed, but without particular character, except that they carried an air of importance and good-living. A third man held

Kirby's interest. He was big and fleshy, but his flesh was hard. He was tanned and the bulges in his short neck were muscular. He wore a dark sack suit, but with a touch of Indian color. He had a wide-brimmed hat with a beaded band. He also had a beaded belt and Crow-made moccasins.

Despite this, Kirby decided there was no Indian blood in him. The touch of the exotic was for effect.

The fourth man who had brought up the rear was remarkable for his utter lack of color. He was a cadaverously thin person, with clean-shaven, pallid features that were blank of expression. He wore a knee-length black plantation coat, a black vest of watered silk and a starched white shirt and gates ajar collar with a small black bow tie. He also had a brace of six-shooters beneath the skirts of his coat.

"The flashy one," Ray Coleman murmured, "is Barney Inchman. Ever hear of him?"

"No," Kirby said.

"You will if you go into the railroad business," Coleman said. "He calls himself a promoter. He's a thief."

Barney Inchman bought a bottle of good whisky at the bar. Carrying it, he led the way to a table near where Kirby and

Coleman sat. Only two of his companions joined him. The cadaverous man preferred to sit in at a poker table just to Kirby's right.

Barney Inchman discovered Coleman's presence and made an expansive gesture. "Hello there, Coleman!" he boomed so that everyone in the room could hear.

Ray Coleman's response was without warmth. "Howdy!"

"Inchman's the kind of a sharpshooter who'd skin you out of your boots in a blizzard," Coleman told Kirby. "He's been trying to wedge himself into a piece of the Union Pacific. He talked them into letting him represent them in selling stock back East. They found out he was keeping the money. I understand that Dr. Durant, who is the big man in U.P., had him thrown out of his parlor car today."

He went on, "Inchman had Horace Logan believing in him too. Logan would give his right arm to he named general manager of the U.P. Or president. But that's over. He's tarred with the same brush as Inchman, at least as far as Dr. Durant is concerned. I've got a hunch Inchman played Logan for a sucker. At any rate, the general is distinctly out in the cold as far as the Union Pacific and Dr.

Durant are concerned."

"Apparently you and Inchman have rubbed fur at times."

Coleman smiled. "He knows what I think of him."

He added, "But Inchman is dangerous. Make no mistake about that. He can use a gun, if need be. And his fists. He's had a checkered career. Prize fighter, bouncer in honky-tonks, confidence man, promoter. He has a gift for stealing big money, and staying out of prison. He doesn't have to do any more killing. He's got Parson Slate around to take care of chores like that, if need be."

"Parson Slate?"

"The walking skeleton that came in with them who's now playing poker just to your right. Slate's a gunman. A killer. He's Inchman's personal bodyguard. Inchman sometimes has more of them around, but Slate is always with him. Slate is said to have been a preacher and came West for his health. I know for a fact that he is a narcotic addict. Morphine."

"How did a man like Horace Logan get mixed up with them?" Kirby asked. "To give the devil his due, I can't figure Logan as being a financial crook."

"Inchman's a glib salesman. It's my

guess that he used the general's war record as a front to try to put over his own schemes. He failed to fool Dr. Durant, at least."

Ray Coleman had been doing a lot of talking for a man who usually preferred to be a listener. He lovingly fingered his spike-point mustache, testing the wax.

"Someday I'm going to shave the damned thing off," he said. "I spend half my time keeping it looking nice."

Kirby realized that his companion was trying to divert his mind from the purpose that had brought him to Omaha. Coleman was stalling for time while he searched for some plan that would sway Kirby from his intention of confronting Horace Logan.

Kirby's head suddenly lifted. Coleman twisted in his chair to peer. A newcomer had entered the gambling house. A young, quietly garbed man in a linen jacket. The left sleeve of the jacket was empty and pinned up. Reid Logan.

Chapter 4

Reid Logan had a pistol thrust in his belt in plain sight at the front of his open coat. He stood scanning the room. He had a striking likeness to his sister. The same hue of hair and eye, the same pride of bearing.

He singled out Kirby and came walking down the room.

Kirby spoke softly to Coleman. "There might be trouble. Better move away from me."

Coleman, surprised, started to push his chair back, then paused. "Are you armed, Kirby?"

"No. My gun is in my possible bag at the steamboat office."

"Well, I've got a gun," Coleman said. "I'll stay here."

However, Reid Logan made no move to draw as he approached. He halted at their table and looked at Kirby. "I followed you all the way from Lockport, McCabe. I just got here on a steamboat that I caught shortly after you left St. Louis. I've been searching the town for you."

"So you found me," Kirby asked. "Why?"

"You know why. If you make a move to harm my father, I'll kill you. That's your answer."

He started to move away. And halted. Another arrival had appeared in the Four Aces. His father.

Horace Logan's mustache and beard had turned steel gray since Kirby had last seen him at inspection before the Battle at Shiloh. His stern face was drawn and seamed. It was also ashen. His gaze was fixed on Barney Inchman's group. There was a wild glare in his eyes. He was unshaven and hatless, his hair unkempt, his necktie askew.

He had a Colt Navy pistol in a holster that was strapped outside his cutaway coat. It was the same weapon he had carried as a military commander.

He strode down the length of the gambling house, his tortured eyes fixed on Inchman. He seemed oblivious of anything else. He apparently did not know that his son was in the place. He had the look of a man driven to desperation.

Inchman seemed unaware of Horace Logan's presence until one of his companions looked up and uttered a startled warning. However, Kirby had the impression that Inchman's surprise was forced. The man

59

had been expecting something like this.

Horace Logan paused two strides away. "Get on your feet, Inchman," he said. "If you've got a gun, use it. If you haven't, I'll see that you're furnished with one. You disgraced my good name, tricked me into being branded as a schemer and a swindler like yourself. I want satisfaction."

Inchman sat motionless, his shrewd eyes sizing up the situation, assaying his chances. He was cool enough. "I don't want to fight you, Logan," he said. "Be sensible. Turn around and go away."

Reid Logan was staring, apparently stunned by this turn of events. He saw, no doubt, that any attempt to interfere might only touch off a gunfight.

"Get up and fight, or crawl on your belly and admit you lied to me from start to finish," Horace Logan said hoarsely.

Kirby saw Inchman's glance dart briefly in another direction. And flash a message. The person with whom Inchman had communicated was the saturnine poker player at the table near Kirby. Parson Slate.

Kirby guessed what was coming. Reid Logan must have guessed it also. Both of them moved before Inchman put into motion the strategy he had planned.

Inchman plunged from his chair toward Horace Logan in a maneuver that appeared that he was making a bold attempt to overpower an armed man who had all the advantage.

At the same moment Parson Slate rose from his chair at the poker table. A six-shooter was in his hand. He swung the weapon high and began the deadly down-chop which would end in the hurling of a bullet that would take Horace Logan in the back across the room.

Reid Logan's motion was instinctive to shield his father — a lunging dive that spilled a bystander from his feet at the birdcage game, sending the man sprawling. But Reid Logan would never have made the distance across the room in time.

Kirby was the nearest to Parson Slate, the only one who had a chance of preventing Horace Logan from being shot down. His action was also instinctive — almost a muscular reflex. He had no time to think, no time to reason that this was not his affair. No time to remember that he, by rights, should be the last man on earth to intervene in Horace Logan's behalf. But he acted.

He only partly succeeded. His shoulder struck Parson Slate at the waist as the gunman fired. He carried the man with him and they crashed heavily to the sawdust. The gun was knocked from Slate's hand.

Slate fought with fierce strength for an instant, trying to break free. Then, suddenly, he was spent. Kirby rammed an elbow into him, and he sagged back, gagging.

Kirby arose, kicking Slate's pistol far away beneath the tables among men who had ducked for cover.

Horace Logan was reeling, clutching a table for support. Blood was staining his coat at the back where Slate's bullet had found him.

His son stood shielding him from Inchman, who had a derringer in his hand. But, most of all, Reid Logan was shielding his father from Parson Slate, who was trying to draw his other six-shooter. Kirby snatched away the weapon and sent it skidding across the sawdust.

For a moment it was a still tableau. Inchman stood crouched, waiting. Reid Logan's six-shooter bore on the man's stomach at point-blank range. Nobody moved. Every person in the room was awaiting the blast of gunfire that seemed inevitable, and which would almost certainly mean the deaths of both Inchman and Reid Logan.

A girl's scream sounded. She had entered from the swing doors and was racing frantically down the room.

She was Norah Logan. She reached her father and supported him. "Help me, Reid!" she gasped.

That broke the spell. Reid Logan holstered his pistol and helped lift his father on a poker table. Horace Logan seemed to be badly wounded, for his head sagged, and Kirby could see the whites of his eyes.

"A doctor!" Norah Logan screamed. "Someone get a doctor!" Men were rising to their feet and beginning to mill about. Others were crowding in from the street, staring and asking questions.

Kirby glanced around. Slate had slipped away. He glimpsed the gunman fighting his way out of the door through the stream of incoming men. Because of the confusion, there was little hope of intercepting him.

Kirby dusted sawdust from his clothing. Ray Coleman joined him. He endured Coleman's quizzical stare for a time. "All right," he finally said waspishly. "I made a fool of myself."

"I'd hardly call it that," Coleman said.

"But you *could* have got yourself killed. Why?"

"I'm wondering myself," Kirby admitted. "Maybe I figured Horace Logan didn't deserve to die that easy. Maybe I wanted to pull the trigger myself."

Coleman shrugged. "You'll never do that. You're not a killer, Kirby." He added, "Thank God, you never will be, now. Horace Logan looks like he's in bad shape."

Horace Logan lay moaning on the table while his daughter and son used towels that bartenders brought in an attempt to stem the blood. Presently a doctor came hurrying in. Another medical man arrived a few minutes later. A town marshal appeared and began asking disinterested questions.

Norah Logan gave way to the two medical men. She stepped back and singled out Kirby, appraising him as though puzzled. She said something to her brother.

Reid Logan hesitated, then approached Kirby. "They say you knocked down the man who shot my father."

"It seems that I did," Kirby said. He started to turn away.

Reid Logan halted him. "I don't understand."

"Understand what?"

"I'd hardly expect you to interfere in a thing like that. Not to help my father, at least. I believed it would be the other way around."

"Maybe I don't like to see people shot in the back," Kirby said. "Not even a Logan."

Reid Logan studied him. "Nothing's changed, is it?" he said. "Not really changed."

"No," Kirby said.

"You know why I'm here, McCabe. Nothing's changed in that respect either."

Kirby nodded. "Thanks for the warning."

"I still don't understand why you interfered. My father probably would be dead already if you hadn't taken a hand."

"Maybe it was too early for him to die. There're matters to be settled with him."

Kirby moved away. Reid Logan stood debating whether to continue the discussion, then decided against it.

Ray Coleman followed Kirby. "Who is the young lady?"

"Logan's daughter," Kirby said.

"Why is she here?"

"I believe she and her brother came to Omaha to kill me, if necessary."

"What?"

"The Logans stand together. It's for the sake of their family pride. They want the ghosts of Shiloh to stay buried. They know I intend to rattle the bones. That will destroy the Logans. At least their pride."

Lee and Stella Venters, who had been assuring the patrons the trouble was over, now joined Kirby and Coleman. "This is the first shooting we've had in the Aces in a long time," Lee sighed.

"I refuse to let it spoil our reunion," Stella said. "You two haven't forgotten that you're to have supper with us?"

"Maybe you'd prefer to put it off," Coleman said.

"No. I insist. I've sent word to Timmy to be sure to have apple pie and ice cream."

"Ice cream? You wouldn't fool a man, would you?"

"Real ice cream, sir. Made by Timmy. The ice is brought by boat from St. Louis. Can't you realize that civilization is moving West? Why, you can order oysters from New Orleans at the New York House right across the street. And terrapin soup from Maryland."

"But ice cream," Coleman said reverently. "That is from heaven."

"You'll have some as soon as Lee can come with us," she promised.

A deputy marshal approached and looked Kirby over. "Did you know the fella that shot the general?" he asked.

"Never laid eyes on him before," Kirby said.

The lawman evidently didn't believe him, but had no interest in making an issue of it. "Folks generally ain't in the habit of messin' into gunfights among strangers," he commented, and went away.

A stretcher was brought and Horace Logan was carried away, accompanied by his son and daughter.

"The Union Pacific has a hospital here," Stella explained. "They'll take him there, no doubt."

"How does he seem to be making out?" Coleman asked Lee.

Lee Venters shrugged. "I'd say he'll be lucky to hang on 'til they get him to the hospital. He's in bad shape."

Inchman and his companions had left, after being questioned by the marshal. "What about Parson Slate?" Coleman asked.

"What can the marshal do? Logan was threatening Inchman. Inchman told the marshal he owes his life to Slate. He claims Slate only intended to shoot into the roof to scare Logan and that whoever knocked him down really was the one responsible for the general being hit."

"That," Kirby said, "would be me."

"It will be put down as an accident," Lee said.

The Four Aces was resuming normal activity. The roulette ball began rolling. Cards were dealt at the poker tables.

Lee Venters pulled the cover over his faro table. "Back in an hour or so, gentlemen," he said to bystanders.

He and his wife led Kirby and Coleman out of the place. The Venters residence turned out to be an ark-like structure mounted on the wheels and frames of two freight wagons. It stood in a vacant lot not far from the railroad yards on the fringe of town.

"Welcome to Rolling Stone Manor," Lee said. "Here today and gone tomorrow. Like the Four Aces, we can be wheeled aboard a flatcar on an hour's notice."

The exteriors had been painted a warm gray, with windows and doors trimmed in gay yellow. There were window flower boxes, and a small porch as well as a stoop and steps at the door of what proved to be the kitchen.

The living room was small but cozily furnished with rag rugs and calico curtains. Easy chairs stood waiting.

"We figure we'll have to move every few months," Stella explained. "So we decided to be comfortable and carry our home along with us."

A slender, comely girl with fine light hair, came from the kitchen, flushed and flustered.

Kirby stared. "Who in blazes are you?"

She pouted. "You know very well who I am. You promised to marry me when I grew up. Well, I'm grown up."

Kirby kissed Timothea Venters. "This can't be real," he said. "Why it wasn't more'n a month or so ago in Denver that you were in pigtails and bucking like a steer at having to wear shoes when your mother was sending you off to school."

"That was a long time ago," Timmy sniffed. "More than two years. You didn't expect me to be a child all my life, did you?"

"I could think of worse things."

"So you're not going to keep your promise," she said, pretending scorn.

"I'd likely be killed in the stampede," Kirby said. "I've got a hunch there'll be a herd of poor devils pawing the air and locking horns for the chance of holding hands with a certain taffy-haired party."

Timmy laughed, pleased, and made a face at him. She had been born on a Mississippi River packet. Her mother had been a singer who entertained passengers in the first cabin of the *Natchez Belle*. Her father had been a young hotspur in the dueling, gambling circles of New Orleans when he had married the beautiful river boat singer.

Gambling was in Lee Venters' nature. Timmy had spent her childhood on packets, sharing the plush days when her parents were in funds, and the threadbare intervals when the cards ran the wrong way.

Lee had headed West with his wife and daughter when the Pikes Peak gold rush started. But his luck was not the kind that finds raw gold. He had returned to the skill he knew best. He became the owner of a gambling house in Denver which he named the Four Aces. It developed a reputation for straight dealing.

Stella had continued to operate the Four Aces after her husband left to fight on the side of the Confederacy. The fame of the place had spread. The beauty of the coppery-haired faro dealer became legendary with the telling and retelling. It became a matter of prestige to have sat in a game dealt by the gorgeous and virtuous Stella

Venters at the Four Aces in Denver City.

This same legendary Stella Venters was now bustling around with housewifely energy, taking charge of finishing off preparations for the supper Timmy and the housekeeper had under way. She saw to it that drinks were served and that Kirby and Ray Coleman had the best of the armchairs. She patted her husband's cheek with affection.

"Again we say you're a lucky man," Coleman told Lee.

"I've had more'n my fair share, I reckon," Lee said. "But luck never runs one way forever. We aim to have a stake by the time the railroad is finished so that we can buy into somethin' besides a gamblin' house. A store, maybe."

"I can't picture you back of a counter in a store," Kirby commented. "Nor Stella. She seems to thrive on this sort of life."

"I'm afeared Timmy does too," Lee admitted. "But it ain't fair to her. We run honest games, but cards just naturally seem to breed trouble. That shootin' tonight wasn't the first one we've had in spite of everythin' we do to avoid such things."

He added, "But who'd have figured that a man as important as Horace Logan would go on the kill, an' get himself shot. Why, there was talk the President of the United States had telegraphed a message to him lately, offerin' to make him an ambassador to one of them foreign countries."

"Maybe to mollify him for the way Dr. Durant was squashing him when he tried to force his way into the inner circles of the Union Pacific," Coleman commented. "It was a sour pill for the general to swallow, so I understand. That's why he went on the prod, evidently."

Stella called them to the table. It was a homey meal, Southern-style. Fried chicken, yams, hominy grits, biscuits, chicory coffee. And, as promised, real ice cream, served with dried apple pie. They had finally leaned back in the chairs and the men had lighted smokes when a hand tapped the door.

Timmy hurried to answer the door. It was a feminine voice that spoke. "I would like to speak to Mr. McCabe."

Kirby turned, then got to his feet. The caller was Norah Logan. She had wrapped a light cloak around her shoulders and wore a poke bonnet that shadowed her face. The lamplight reached her features. She was worn and tired.

"I came here to tell you, Mr. McCabe, that you won't have to hound my father any longer," she said shrilly. "At least my brother has been spared the need of killing you. My father's beyond harm now. I'm thankful for that, at least. You should be thankful, too, that it's all over. I was told I'd find you here."

So Horace Logan was dead!

Norah Logan started to turn away. She paused and spoke again. "I tell you for the last time you were wrong about him that day at Shiloh. What he did was his duty."

Kirby spoke. "And was it his duty to try to put the blame on a man he probably thought was dead and would never be able to speak for himself?"

She considered that for a moment. "At any rate, it's finished now."

She descended the steps and walked away through the darkness. She had come alone.

Timmy closed the door. Nobody spoke for a time. Kirby finally looked at Ray Coleman. "Is that offer still open? In California?"

Coleman brightened. "Very much so. Do you mean it?"

"There's nothing to keep me here any longer," Kirby said.

"I'm catching a work train at five o'clock in the morning that will take me to the end of track," Coleman said. "From there I'm taking a Western Mail stage to Fort Kearny and connect there with the Overland Mail to California. Can you make it in the morning?"

"I can make it," Kirby said.

Timmy cried out in protest. "We'll never see you again!"

Kirby put an arm around her. "Of course you will. You're going West with the railroad. We'll build east with the Central Pacific. They'll meet somewhere. Halfway across, I suppose."

"You'll wait for me?"

Kirby chucked her under the chin. "No. And you will not wait for me, either, young lady."

Chapter 5

Kirby stood on top of the cab of a bell-stacked Central Pacific locomotive that overlooked a gathering of men, all of whom had suddenly grown utterly silent.

Every eye was on two men who stood with silver mallets poised above a golden spike that was to be driven into a polished railroad tie made of California laurel.

The day was May 10, 1869. Nearly three years had passed since the night he and Ray Coleman had said goodbye to the Venters at Omaha. He was stalwart now, rather than lank. A big, sinewy man. The crow's-feet had deepened at his mouth and eyes. He bore the hallmark of responsibility, of authority. Men like Leland Stanford and Dr. Thomas C. Durant, who were the ones poising the silver mallets, used his first name when they spoke to him.

Hard rock drillers and blasting experts in the construction crews that had built the Central Pacific over the mountains, across the Nevada desert and to this meeting with the Union Pacific at Promontory Point in Utah, often saluted him when they spoke.

The Chinese coolies who had helped build the C.P. by sweat and muscle power, bowed respectfully when he passed by.

Jack Casement, construction boss of the Union Pacific, waved from the opposite engine. They gripped their hands above their heads in mutual exhilaration. The great task was finished.

A mallet descended. A telegraph operator, whose sounder was hooked to the spike, said, "One!"

The second mallet descended. "Two!"

All over the nation sounders were recording the blows on the spike. Cannon would now be booming in Washington, in Sacramento, in San Francisco and New York. The nation was linked from coast to coast with steel.

The cheering began and welled to wild screeching. The champagne began flowing. Chinese coolies who had graded roadbed at a pace of ten miles a day beneath a blistering sun, stood grinning beneath their round hats, not exactly understanding that they were now adrift, aliens in an alien land and that they would no longer have the big, hard-fisted, black-haired Kirby McCabe to look after them and protect them from the dislike of the tarriers on the steel gangs.

Kirby drank champagne. He shook hands with Governor Stanford and Dr. Durant and Jack Casement. And Granville Dodge. The 21st U.S. Infantry band tried to make itself heard amid the uproar, but gave up when champagne was poured down the brass throats of the instruments.

Irish paddies from Casement's crews embraced their counterparts from the Central Pacific.

"They're so friendly now, it's sickening," Jack Casement said to Kirby. "Before the night's over, when they get their hides full of whisky, there's going to he hell to pay. I've warned every gang boss and special officer to stay sober and stand by to stop riots."

"I've done the same," Kirby said. "Pride is wonderful — and leads to a poke in the nose when they start telling how much more steel they laid in a day than the other outfit."

Casement grinned. "Too bad Ray Coleman isn't here. I understand he's in South America."

Kirby nodded. "At least he should be, although I haven't heard a word. He pulled out about six months ago. But Chile is a long, long distance away and Ray never was much of a letter writer. He had a good offer from the people down there who are building a railroad across the Andes. His work with the Central Pacific was finished anyway."

"That's the sort of thing Ray loves," Casement said. "New scenes, new engineering problems to tackle. Can't blame him. I feel like a kid who'd lost his last marble today. This has been fun, building this damned choo-choo line. But it's finished. It's as though I'd just buried an old friend."

"Speaking of old friends, how about the Venters?" Kirby asked. "Lee and Stella? And Timmy? Did they follow your camps all the way West with their Four Aces?"

"They did. They made their last stand in Ogden. But they knocked down their place several weeks ago, loaded it on a flatcar and headed East."

Kirby was disappointed. "I'd hoped to see them. It's been a long time. Back in Omaha."

"Both Lee and Mrs. Venters asked me to convey their regards to you," Casement said. "They said they hoped you would meet them somewhere in the near future."

"I'm afraid there's little chance of that. I've made up my mind to join Ray Coleman in Chile. He told me when he left that there'd be a job waiting for me down there."

"The young lady also asked to be remembered to you."

"Timmy? How is she?"

"A raving beauty. She had broken the hearts of all the young engineers on my staff. She told me to inform you that she has given up hope of winning you and will wait no longer."

Kirby laughed. "So I've been cast aside. Timmy will be nineteen now, or twenty. And still not married. I take it her father is quitting the gambling business."

"Why do you say that?"

"He told me at Omaha that he aimed to go into something else after the railroad was built."

"A gambler never quits. You know that, Kirby. No more than you can quit breathing of your own free will. It's Stella's nature also, to buck the tiger. They were heading for a new end of steel to do it all over again."

"A new end of steel? A new railroad?"

"You've heard of the Grand Pacific, haven't you?"

"Yes. You mean there's really something to that?"

"Very much so. At least the Grand Pacific has sold a lot of stock back East and is spending the money. They've bought a small railroad that was built across the Iowa prairie to the Missouri River, and another line east of the Mississippi so as to give them an outlet to Chicago. They've already spent millions. They mean business."

"They're really planning to build all the way to the Pacific Coast?"

"They say they'll cross Dakota Territory and Montana to the Columbia River and be in Portland in two years," Casement said.

"That's quite a chore. The Sioux might have something to say about it. That's their buffalo country. The Cheyennes have a stake up there also, and are mighty touchy about it."

"Indians or not, I understand the G.P. is starting to grade west of the Missouri River. Their base is a new settlement named Antler in Dakota Territory."

Casement added with a sigh, "I can't say I blame the Venters. If I wasn't tied up with other commitments, danged if I wouldn't go there and take a look myself. In fact I had a good offer some months ago from Horace Logan to throw in with him in building the line. I turned it down, of course. Logan was mixed up in a scheme to get control of the Union Pacific a few years ago. It didn't smell too good, although I've been told that he was only being used as a front —"

He paused, realizing that Kirby was staring at him excitedly. "Logan?" Kirby spoke. "Did you say the name was *Horace* Logan?"

"Why, yes," Casement said. "The Civil War general."

Kirby found his voice shaking. "But Horace Logan is dead! I saw him shot in Omaha back in the early days of the U.P."

"I recall that he was mixed up in a gun scrape back there," Casement said. "But he pulled through. If we're talking about the same man, he's very much alive. He's finally got what he wanted. The job of bossing a big railroad."

Casement peered closer at Kirby. "What's wrong? You look like you might be seeing a ghost!"

"That's exactly what I am seeing," Kirby said.

So Norah Logan had tricked him that night in Omaha when she had led him to believe her father had died of his wound. It was plain enough. She had deluded him in order to gain time until her father could be

81

moved out of his reach.

His departure the following morning for California with Ray Coleman had no doubt made a far greater success of her deception than she had anticipated.

California had been another world. The hectic task of smashing right-of-way across the Sierra Nevada, and the race for mileage through the desert to meet the steel that Casement's Union Pacific crews were laying, had occupied his thoughts and his time. He had rarely seen Eastern newspapers. If Horace Logan's name had appeared in any of them, or in any of the Sacramento and San Francisco newspapers, he had overlooked it.

Even though he had not received word from Ray Coleman since the older man's departure for South America nearly six months earlier, Kirby had arranged passage for Valparaiso, Chile, on a vessel that was scheduled to weigh anchor at San Francisco in about three weeks. His work with Central Pacific was finished, and while a good position had been offered him it seemed to mean nothing but routine work in contrast to the task of conquering the Andes.

Communication with Chile was subject to the uncertainties of sailing schedules and Kirby was not troubled by the long delay in hearing from his friend. Ray Coleman, no doubt, was up to his ears in his new responsibility, and he was a lax letter writer, at best. Ray had said that building a railroad across the Andes might take ten years. It was a challenge, and Kirby had been anxious to join Ray in the battle.

Suddenly all this was swept away. Horace Logan was alive! Kirby surmised that Ray Coleman must have known this and had probably led a conspiracy among those around them to keep the news from him all these years.

The twenty-nine still slept in their graves at Shiloh and there had been no one to speak for them. The accusation that he had brought the rebel cannon down on the remainder of the regiment was still unrefuted. It rose before him now in all its ugliness. Time had failed to absolve the sins of the battlefield.

He stood debating it. The easy way would be to let the ghosts stay buried. In Chile he would be almost on the other side of the planet. He would never have to go back to Lockport to face the scorn in the eyes of its people.

He left Casement and walked to the cubbyhole that had been assigned to him in a bunk car to serve as his office. He sat gazing unseeingly at his reflection in the warped shaving mirror above his desk. His face bore the scars of the years. Also his fists. As camp boss, dealing with tough, primitive men, he had just his fists at times. On one occasion the weapon he had been forced to wield had been a six-shooter.

That gunfight had nothing in common with the battle at Shiloh or campaigning against the Indians. War was mechanical, a matter of shadows and distance. The opposition had been unreal, and there had been only the need for his own survival.

The duel had been starkly personal with his own life depending on his speed. The other man had been a border ruffian who had forced the issue in an attempt to build up a reputation as a bad man. Kirby had lived and the ruffian had died. But that encounter had left scars that went deeper than surface marks.

This reflection in the mirror was what was called maturity, forged by close contact with life and its challenges, by familiarity with death and the knowledge of how frail is the line between the two.

There could be no easy way with him.

Not with the pledge he had made to the twenty-nine still unfulfilled. Not with the stain Horace Logan had placed on his name still raw and ugly.

He began clearing out his desk, closing out his official duties. These formalities took time.

It was two days later when he singled out a personal letter from a batch of mail that had been placed before him. The postmark on the envelope was that of Antler, T.D. Territory of Dakota. It was dated weeks in the past. It had been addressed to him at his Sacramento office, and had undergone many forwardings, many delays.

It had been written by Lee Venters:

Dear Kirby:
It's been a long time since we've bent elbows together. There's some kind of skulduggery going on here that has to do with the building of the Grand Pacific. Our old friend, Ray Coleman, seems to be mixed up in it. I haven't been able to get hold of Ray personally to get the straight of it, but there's a big skunk downwind as sure as I'm a foot high.
Horace Logan is the big augur in the G.P. You never told me what was back

of that business in Omaha that night but I could see that Logan had dealt you some marked cards in the past.

Regardless of Logan, I'm worried about Ray Coleman. I can't believe he'd be in on anything crooked, but it sure looks bad for him. I've got a hunch I know what's in the wind. If so, it's too big for one man to handle. I need help and advice. If you could make a swing to Antler I'd sure like to talk to you.

Your friend,
Lee Venters

Kirby read the letter again, puzzled and incredulous. What was Lee talking about? It was impossible, of course. Raymond Coleman was in South America.

Or should be. There was the snag. Lee said Ray was in Dakota Territory. And Lee seemed positive. And there was the six-month lapse since Kirby had heard from his friend.

Skulduggery! And Lee said Ray was mixed up in it. Lee *must* be mistaken. After all, his letter said he hadn't talked to Ray personally.

At any rate Kirby now had a double reason for heading for Antler. Within twenty-four hours he was eastbound over the Union Pacific. His passage to South America had been canceled. He was on his way to Antler.

It was sundown of a warm June day when he stepped from the sternwheeler that had brought him up the Missouri River from Omaha on the last leg of his trip to Antler.

And it was Omaha all over again. The Omaha of the days when the Union Pacific was starting to push steel westward. Omaha, even to the mud. Although the weather was clear at the moment, rains had been sweeping the plains and the Missouri River was high and carrying far more than its customary load of mud.

Antler stood on the west bank of the river, and pile drivers were hammering the posts of a trestle that would link it permanently with rails that had crossed the prairie to the stream. Meanwhile, ferries and barges were moving humans and supplies back and forth across the river.

This was a silk hat and buckskin town. Buffalo hides stank on the levee, waiting shipment, and the same steamboat that would load the hides was now ridding itself of a grand piano and of packing boxes and crates of bric-a-brac.

Frock coats rubbed shoulders with the homespun of bullwhackers. The fragrance of fine Havana cigars mingled with the rank tang of kinnikinnick from the corncob pipes of trappers. They all moved along the duckboard sidewalks through which the mud of the Dakota country squished and spurted to stain boots and moccasins.

And slippers. The fancy women were here, to be sure, picking their way along and berating men who did not respect their sex on the crowded pathways. Only the Pawnees and Kaws walked always in the mud. Sidewalks were not for Indians, even those who had made their peace with the whites.

The knockdown gambling houses and honky-tonks and the mobile mercantiles were set along a crooked principal street that was named Lincoln Street. The majority of these structures were freshly spruced-up, but paint did not cover all the scars of their service on the Union Pacific. Of Julesburg, Cheyenne, Rock Springs, Echo, Ogden. These were their badges of membership in the ribald, roaring fraternity of the gypsy towns, the moving hell-holes that had followed the end of steel along the Overland Trail.

Now they were poised to whoop their

way through the Dakota country. Only the insignia on the locomotives that puffed in the railroad yards, and on the machine shops was different. It now read: *Grand Pacific.*

Grand Pacific steel was pushing west. And west lay the Sioux country. Treaty country where the northern buffalo herd was yet to know the real roar of the big Sharps fifties in the hands of the hide hunters. Virgin country.

Kirby left his luggage at the steamboat baggage office and walked up the crowded street. This was Boom Town again — but with a difference.

There were too many silk hats and white collars. Not all of the feminine figures were fancy women. Oh, they looked pretty enough. Expensive rather. They seemed to be swarming like bees. Their focal point appeared to be the biggest structure in town, a hotel named the Dakota House.

"What's going on?" Kirby asked a bearded oldster who had a bullwhip coiled over his shoulder and carried a Bowie knife in a scabbard on his belt. "Some of these people look like they belong about two thousand miles east of here."

The bullwhacker gave a cackle of amusement. "Them's Eastern lob bellies, sure enough. The pure, distilled strain. Noses so high in the air they kin see right down their backbones. Smell that stink? Perfume. It'll drive all the game out'n the country fer a hundred miles, skin my hide if it won't."

"What are they doing here?"

"Gineral Logan brung 'em. A whole trainload of 'em, like cattle. The G.P.'s footin' the bill, so they think. But I'll reckon they'll be the ones that pay for the shindig after the general shakes a couple more million dollars out'n their wallets to throw down a rathole."

"Rathole?"

The man gave him a second look and decided not to be talkative to a stranger. "It's a fur piece to Oregon," he said. "You workin' fer the G.P.?"

"No," Kirby said. "So General Logan is here in person? Here in Antler?"

He was again inspected before he got an answer. "He's fixin' to make a big speech at a banquet the day after tomorrow. It's to be a real he-diller of a feed. Why, they say a feller's down in the ice house, carvin' out figgers o' women from cakes of ice which they're goin' to use to cool the champagne."

The man paused and spat. "Neked

90

women!" he added scathingly. "A pack o' heathens, I say. Rollin' in money an' sin!"

There must have been upward of a hundred Easterners taking in the sights of the town. It was an inspection trip, and, as the bullwhacker had said, its purpose was to interest the visitors in investing in Grand Pacific stock. Such excursions had been standard practice with both the Union Pacific and Central Pacific and Kirby had undergone a couple of experiences with such junkets.

The visitors would be wined and dined. The wild West would he paraded before them as they sipped champagne or gazed from the many carriages that were carrying them along the street.

An Indian ceremonial drum began booming on a show ground off the main thoroughfare. A big tent had been pitched there for the benefit of the visitors. Feathered tribesmen and squaws began preparations for their dance. The Easterners were flocking toward this point of interest.

Torchlights blazed. They illuminated gaudy banners at the medicine shows and honky-tonks. A girl dancer was prancing on a platform in front of a music hall. Music blared, hurdy-gurdies tinkled, barkers chanted their spiels.

A party of laughing, talkative Easterners, returning from a sightseeing ride, blocked Kirby's path as they alighted from a four-horse freight wagon that had been fitted with plank seats.

He found himself facing Norah Logan at close range. She started to pass by, then halted, not sure at first that what she was seeing was true. Then she *was* certain. The light-hearted animation faded. Dread came. Then defiance and a challenge.

She was a person easy to read. Three years had brought to full flood her allure, given her poise and added depth to her character. She had instantly judged that his presence here was a danger to her father. She had at once gathered her own inner forces to meet that threat.

Neither of them spoke. She gazed at him as though trying to pick his mind and learn his immediate intentions. She failed. He could see the dread increase.

She turned abruptly away, took the arm of one of the men in the party and joined the others who were streaming toward where the Pawnees had started their dance. War whoops were rising as the Indians warmed to the entertainment.

Kirby moved on down the street. He

presently sighted the structure he had hoped to find. The Four Aces. Stepping through its door was like stepping back to the night Horace Logan had been shot. The same atmosphere of professional calm, the same type of players, the same restrained call of the croupiers.

There was one difference. The faro table stood in its customary place in the center of the gambling line, but it was Stella Venters who sat in the dealer's chair. A man was taking care of the case.

Stella wore black. There were shadows under her eyes. Marks of grief and sadness. Kirby felt a chill. Stella was in mourning.

She glanced up. He had the impression his appearance was no surprise to her. It was as though she had looked up many times, expecting him — and hoping he would never come through those swing doors.

Her eyes rested squarely on him for an instant. He started to speak and moved toward her. Then he halted, the words fading. Her eyes remained blank. She returned to her task at the table, drawing another card from the box.

She had refused to recognize him, refused to offer any sign that she was aware of his presence.

Chapter 6

Kirby, puzzled, moved to the bar. "Beer," he said. "If it's cold."

"Mister," the bartender said, "Antler's got its own ice plant. Yes sir, this town is on its way. The only cold beer in two hundred miles."

Stella Venters did not look in Kirby's direction. At first he tried to tell himself that perhaps she really hadn't recognized him. But he soon knew this was not so. She knew he was there.

There was some dark shadow in her. Greater than the sadness, even greater than the grief. Terror. She was deathly afraid. Of what? She was afraid to acknowledge his presence.

Kirby appraised the players at the games. All were strangers. There was nothing here from the past that would give him a clue to the reason for her attitude.

And where was her husband? The chill increased inside Kirby. Lee Venters was dead. He was sure of it.

The beer was cold enough. But he left it half-finished. He had lost his taste for it.

He walked out of the Four Aces and began looking for a place to put up for the night.

He decided to try the Dakota House, but the clerk only gave him a bored look and said, "We're loaded with General Logan's party. I've turned down twenty persons in the last hour. I doubt if you'll find quarters in Antler tonight, short of a hayloft."

As he turned to leave, Kirby slowed his pace. A big, heavy-shouldered man was sitting in the hotel parlor to the right. He had a flower in the buttonhole of his tailored sack suit and was smoking a good cigar. He was in conversation with a well-dressed companion who wore a gold watchchain with a diamond fob.

The big man was Barney Inchman. It was Omaha all over again. Inchman seemed to be prosperous and as important of manner as the night Horace Logan had challenged him to a gunfight.

And Parson Slate was still Inchman's shadow — his bodyguard. The thin gunman, somberly and neatly garbed as in the past, sat nearby, scanning a newspaper.

Kirby had not been seen by Inchman or Parson Slate. He left the Dakota House and continued his hunt for quarters. Luck was with him. He rented a newly vacated room at his next stop, a second-rate frame structure on a side street. The Buffalo Hotel was the name, and its proprietor went by the improbable handle of Titus Tinker.

His room was at a rear corner of the second floor, overlooking dark freight yards. It was reasonably clean and hot water was available. He brought his luggage from the landing and shaved, bathed and changed to clean linen.

Refreshed, he returned to the Dakota House, having decided that its dining room offered the best chance of a good supper.

The dining room was sparsely filled, for the majority of the guests were still at the Pawnee dance. He was finishing his meal when Inchman and his companion entered and took a table.

Inchman gave Kirby a second look and suddenly lost interest in what the other man was saying. He stared for a moment, then forced himself to turn away. Evidently Inchman remembered him from that night at Omaha. However, the man showed no sign of wanting to reopen the matter. He did not look in Kirby's direction again.

Parson Slate was not in sight, but Kirby became aware of a small, sharp-featured man with a pointed nose, who wandered in almost at Inchman's heels and occupied a table alone. Kirby decided that this was another bodyguard. Inchman seemed to believe he needed constant protection — and had the money to pay for it.

Kirby finished his meal, sat over his coffee for a time, trying to decide his course. He pushed back his chair, paid for his meal and left the hotel, smoking a cigarette.

He strolled along Lincoln Street, drawing deep on the fragrant tobacco, mulling over Stella Venters' attitude. The problem he could not solve was whether he should attempt to see her alone and demand an explanation. He had a hunch she would not tell him the truth.

He found that, without actual purpose, he had headed down a side street away from the blare of the gambling line. Off to the left lay the railroad yards, where switch engines were busy. The rumble of triphammers and the screech of lathes came from the Grand Pacific machine shops farther away.

Eventually, in the starlight loomed an object that was another scene from the past. The migratory home of Lee and Stella Venters.

Rolling Stone Manor, Lee had termed it

that night in Omaha. The night of the apple pie and ice cream. The night Norah Logan had come to its door and had led Kirby to believe her father was dead.

Rolling Stone Manor stood on the fringe of the settlement at a distance from other habitations. It was cheerily lighted, the beams of the lamps reaching onto the flat. He could hear the clink of dishes being washed in the small kitchen.

The outline of the sun-whitened bars of a small pole corral was visible beyond the house, but there was no sign of livestock in the enclosure.

Kirby paused, suddenly at a loss. He realized that, consciously or not, he had been hoping to find the Venters' residence. He tried to decide if he might be breaking faith with Stella by forcing himself into a situation where he was not wanted.

At the moment the belief came to him that he was being watched. Perhaps it had been some sound in the darkness, or merely intuition, but he was suddenly sure that he was in danger.

He was unarmed, having left his six-shooter at the Buffalo Hotel. He felt a chill in his stomach. Timmy abruptly opened the rear door of the kitchen and ran down the steps, carrying a pan of dishwater which she emptied into the soil a distance from the house. The lamplight streamed upon her.

Turning to retrace her steps, she saw Kirby. To her, he was only a menacing shadow. She uttered a scream of fear and raced in panic for the kitchen.

"Timmy!" Kirby called. "It's Kirby McCabe!"

He followed and stood on the steps, looking up at her. She was breathing fast, but she recognized him, and the fear was leaving her.

Kirby looked around. If there really had been anyone shadowing him, Timmy's scream must have given that person a pause.

"Are you all right, Timmy?" Kirby said. "I ought to be shot for giving you such a fright. But, just at that time, I had a feeling that —" He broke off, deciding against mentioning his hunch that he had been followed.

"I thought — I thought — !" Timmy sobbed. Then she drew him into the kitchen and closed the door.

She rushed to him and clung to him. "Oh, I'm so glad!" she choked. "So glad you came. Oh, Kirby, take us away from here. Take Mother away."

Kirby held her against him, soothing her until she calmed. "Where's your father?" he asked gently, fearing the answer.

"Daddy's dead," she sobbed.

"Dead?"

"Murdered! They did it! They —"

Kirby placed a hand over her mouth, silencing her. "No," he said. "I don't want this from you. I want it from your mother . . . if she wants to tell it."

Timmy calmed and looked up at him through swimming eyes. She had all of her mother's cameo beauty, and along with it was her father's dashing spirit and magnetism. "Mother will never tell you. Not because of herself, but —"

"Timmy!" Her mother stood in the door. She was hatless and must have come hurriedly from the faro table, for she still wore the black sleeve guards that she used while at the casino.

"I was afraid you'd come here," she said to Kirby. "To Rolling Stone Manor."

"Then you *did* see me at the Four Aces?" Kirby said.

She didn't answer that. "Go away, Kirby," she said, and there was complete depletion of spirit in her. "You should never have come to Antler. It wasn't fair to — to Timmy."

100

Kirby walked to her, placed his hands on her shoulders, then kissed her. "Lee's dead," he said. "I knew it when I saw you at the Aces."

Stella could only nod. "What happened?" he asked.

"An accident," she said breathlessly. "It was an accident."

"No!" Timmy cried. "It was no accident. It was mur—"

The desperate appeal in her mother's face silenced her. "It *was* an accident," Stella said shakily.

Timmy came to her mother, placed her arms around her and kissed her. In that moment she was the wisest, the one taking the responsibility. "No, Mother," she said. "I know why you're acting this way. It's for me. But you're wrong. Daddy wasn't afraid of them. You wouldn't be afraid of them either if it was only yourself. I don't want it that way."

Her mother tried to stop her, but she turned to Kirby. "There's something wrong with the way they're building the railroad. It's a fraud of some kind."

"Fraud?" Kirby echoed.

"And Raymond Coleman is mixed up in it." Again her mother tried to halt her, but she refused to be silenced. "I eavesdropped on you and Daddy when he was talking about it, and heard him mention Mr. Coleman's name, Mother."

She added, for Kirby's benefit, "I think it has something to do with the route Mr. Coleman located for the railroad."

"The route?" Kirby said. "That's impossible. Ray Coleman never did any locating for the Grand Pacific. He was with the Central Pacific for nearly three —"

He broke off. What did he know about Raymond Coleman's whereabouts these past six months? Really know?

"Mr. Coleman is here in Antler," Timmy said. "I read it in the newspaper."

"What newspaper?"

"In the Antler newspaper that the railroad company has printed here once a week."

"You must be mistaken," Kirby said. "The paper is mistaken."

"Well, all I know is what the paper said. It called him the famous locater who helped decide the route for the Union Pacific. He —"

Kirby halted her and spoke to Stella. "Do you want to finish it for me? Do you want to tell me?"

She was ashen. "I'm sorry you came to Antler, Kirby. I tried to telegraph you to stay away. I didn't know about the letter Lee had sent you until just before he died. He told me, almost with his last breath, to warn you to stay away from Antler."

"Warn me?"

"It was too late. My telegram never reached you. You had already left for Antler."

"You mean Lee was afraid something might happen to me here?" He paused. "Like what happened to him?"

Her silence was her answer.

"Just what *did* happen to Lee?" he asked.

"I tell you it was an accident," she burst out. "We owned a racehorse. A stallion. Lee always had been wild about horse racing. We had it here in the corral back of the house. One evening, after we had finished supper, he went out to make sure everything was all right with the horse before we went back to the Aces. He did that every evening. He was gone unusually long. I found him lying in the corral. He had been kicked in the head. He lived only long enough to tell me to warn you."

"And had he really been kicked by the horse?"

"What else? There were the deep marks of the caulks on his head."

Kirby did not pursue the subject, for he

103

saw that both Stella and Timmy were on the verge of breaking down.

He was reluctant to ask the next question. "What about Ray? Ray Coleman? How is he? Have you talked to him?"

Stella stared at him appealingly, as though praying that he would not push her too far. "I haven't talked to him," she said, her voice very faint.

Kirby drew a long breath. That had been no answer. This was not the time to try to get further information from Stella. He patted her hand. "I can't tell you how sorry I am about Lee," he said. "If you're going back to the Four Aces, Stella, I'll walk with you."

"I'm not going back tonight," she said. "Ben Carhart will take care of the place and bank the game for me. Ben's my assistant. A fine man."

"I'll see you tomorrow, then," Kirby said.

"You mean you're staying?" Stella cried protestingly. "In Antler?"

Kirby studied her. "What is it, Stella?" he demanded. "Why can't you tell me what this is all about? Are you being threatened by someone?"

"What an idea!" she protested. "Who'd threaten me?"

But it didn't ring true. Kirby sensed that he had hit near the truth. Again he saw that it would be cruel to force from her whatever she feared to tell, so he moved to the door.

"Good night," he said.

"Have you got a gun, Kirby?" Stella asked abruptly.

Kirby eyed her. "Not with me. I left it at the hotel. I didn't figure I'd need one."

She moved to a cabinet and opened it. Rifles and fowling pieces were in racks, along with a brace of fine Navy pistols with ivory grips.

She handed him one of the Navys, which was the old-style cap and ball type. "It's primed and capped," she said. "It is one of Lee's guns. I know he'd like you to have it — as a gift."

"Gift?"

"This is a rough town," she said. "People are being bludgeoned by footpads for pennies in their pockets. You *might* need a gun. Goodbye, Kirby."

"Goodbye? That sounds like an invitation never to come back, Stella."

She did not answer. She and Timmy stood in silence as he opened the door and left.

He closed the door and descended the

steps swiftly, then crouched, peering and listening. Stella had not given him the gun merely for defense against footpads. He was sure of that and was remembering his hunch that someone had followed him to Rolling Stone Manor.

He could hear nothing, see nothing. The weedy, brush-clumped flat was silent. No shadow moved. A locomotive whistle hooted dismally in the railroad yards. Sounds of activity in Lincoln Street formed a faint refrain and he heard the trip-hammer in the railroad shops thud heavily, then go silent.

He decided that his fears were ground-less. Nevertheless he had the six-shooter in his hand, his thumb on the hammer, ready for action.

When the shot came he instinctively fired back into the gunflash. Someone had been crouching in the brush fifty yards or more ahead.

His hat was batted from his head by the savage hand of a bullet that had been meant for his brain. He was diving forward on his face, firing again as he went down. He braced himself on his elbows, the pistol ready for more action.

Stella screamed in the house. "Stay where you are!" Kirby shouted. "I'm all right."

He heard the faint sound of someone running away, but was unable to locate the direction. No more shots came. Silence settled. The bushwhacker had fled.

He found his hat. Fifty yards and darkness had been too much of a handicap for the marksman. He had missed, but only by an inch or so.

Men presently came from Lincoln Street to investigate the shooting. One was wearing a badge.

Kirby joined them. "You take part in this shootin' match?" the man with the badge asked.

"I was the target," Kirby said. He poked his finger through the hole in his hat. "I need a new lid. This one will leak real good the next time it rains. My name's McCabe. Kirby McCabe."

"You wouldn't be the McCabe that was whipcracker for the Central Pacific when they was buildin', hell for leather, toward Promontory Point?"

When Kirby confirmed that, the man said, "I've heard of you. Name's Larabee. Jem Larabee. I used to be with the Union Pacific. I'm company detective captain for the Grand Pacific now. A couple of these boys are special officers, workin' for me. Who tried to punch your ticket?"

"I wish I knew," Kirby said. "I'd look him up and take his punch away from him."

Larabee sighed. "That's what they all say. Nobody ever knows anything. Got any witnesses that this other fellow was the first to trip a trigger on you?"

Stella Venters and her daughter had opened the door of their home and had been listening. Stella spoke. "I can testify to that, Mr. Larabee. Mr. Kirby had just left our door, after visiting us. He was a good friend of my husband and had come to pay his respects. The first shot was fired from a distance."

Timmy nodded. "I can testify to that too, Mr. Larabee."

"Thank you, Mrs. Venters," Larabee said respectfully. "An' you too, Miss Timmy." To Kirby he said, "It looks like you got nothin' to worry about, McCabe."

He walked with Kirby to Lincoln Street. When they were alone, he murmured casually, "Or maybe you *ought* to do a little worrying."

"About finding me a new hat?"

"About the head that goes inside it. You've heard the old saw. If at first you don't shoot straight, then try, try ag'in."

"I've heard it," Kirby said. "Do you

108

happen to know a person named Parson Slate?"

Larabee gave him a sidewise look. "I don't know nothin' good about him. But, if you've got any idea it was Slate that took that potshot at you, forget it. Slate was in the Silver Star gambling house at the time I heard the shootin'. He was at his job of ridin' gun herd on a man with money. Barney Inchman. I know this, because I happened to be playin' poker in the same game with Inchman at the time."

"Have Slate and Inchman been in town long?"

"Off an' on since the place was first gettin' its head out o' the mud. Now why would a man like Inchman want you rubbed out?"

"I wouldn't know," Kirby said. "Maybe Inchman's got friends he does favors for."

There really was no sane reason Kirby could think of to link Inchman with the attempt on his life. There was always the possibility that someone from the past who bore him a grudge had recognized him and had decided to settle the score. But he was far more certain it was linked with Lee Venters' murder. Stella's insistence that he be armed had saved his life, no doubt.

"Slate ain't the only gun that looks out

for Barney Inchman's health," Jem Larabee murmured. "There's a pal of Slate's who spells him as a bodyguard. Dried-up little cuss with sharp little eyes an' a pointed nose. Nervous, fidgety. They call him The Sparrow. He's mean. A killer."

"Do you know Raymond Coleman?" Kirby asked abruptly.

"The railroad locater? I know him by sight."

A heaviness and a dark disappointment weighed on Kirby. He had hoped for something different.

"Where can I find him?" he asked.

"Coleman? At the Dakota House, most likely, if he's in town. He spends a lot of time out at the construction camps on Shiloh River to make sure they don't get lost, I reckon."

"Shiloh River?" Kirby echoed. "I never heard of any such river in these parts."

Larabee eyed him with new interest. "Then you ain't a stranger in the Dakota country?"

"Campaigned against the Sioux when I was with the cavalry. There weren't many white men except ourselves around here in those days."

"Shiloh River used to be called Squaw

River," Larabee explained. "General Logan changed the name when they dedicated the cornerstone for the bridge out there. Seems like he did it to honor his son who lost an arm at the Battle of Shiloh."

"They're *bridging* Squaw River? You don't mean they're grading west of the Squaw? They're not locating the railroad in that direction?"

Again Larabee gave him an appraising look. "That seems to be it."

"That means they're building *south* of Squaw Buttes. Are you sure they're not staying this side of the river and swinging north, so that they'll build across the plains north of the buttes?"

"I'm danged sure," Larabee said. "You seem a little ruffled about it. You got different ideas of where they ought to be locatin' this railroad?"

Kirby didn't answer. He was beginning to see it now. The fragments were forming a pattern that was sickeningly alien to his belief in Ray Coleman's integrity.

Skulduggery, Lee Venters had said in his letter. Lee had understated the situation by a wide margin if what Kirby was suspecting turned out to he true. Horace Logan was back of whatever was going on, apparently. But why would he want to destroy the railroad he was promoting?

"If you don't find Coleman at the Dakota House, I reckon General Logan can tell you his whereabouts," Larabee said. "The general's in town, an' that's for sure. He's got a trainload of dudes on his hands to entertain. He's to make a big speech at a fancy banquet two nights from now."

Suddenly Kirby did not want to see Ray Coleman. Not for the present at least.

"I'll look up Coleman later," he said abruptly. "I'd like to go out there, Larabee."

"Out where?"

"To Shiloh River. And maybe farther. Can you deadhead me through on a work train tomorrow?"

Larabee frowned and was suddenly wary. "Just what's in your craw, mister?"

"Maybe I only like to watch steel being spiked down," Kirby said.

"Didn't you see enough of it on the C.P. to last you a lifetime?"

"I'm always interested," Kirby said.

Larabee debated it for a moment. "I reckon I'll tag along, just to make sure about you. You smell like trouble to me. Anyway, nobody goes out to the camps without permission. Mart Garrett has given strict orders against strangers bein' allowed to wander around the right-of-way. Garrett's the front office boss of all construction. Mike Callahan would have you thrown into a baggage car an' shipped back to Antler if you showed up there without authority. Mike's the whipcracker at the steel camp."

"Fair enough," Kirby said. He had decided that Larabee was an honest man. In any event the railroad officer would not stand high enough in Grand Pacific counsels to be in on any chicanery that might be in the making.

"It would be as well if only the two of us knew I was going out there," he added. "I might need a horse when I get out there. I might want to take a look at the country west of the river."

"That can be arranged," Larabee said. "But where you go I go."

"What about the law here?" Kirby asked. "Doesn't anyone care about an attempted murder?"

"You're talkin' to what law there is in Antler," Larabee said. "It's Grand Pacific law. Oh, we got a deputy U.S. marshal around, but he's busy earnin' fees servin' papers for civil suits. Unless somebody gets killed, he's too tied up with paperwork to bother."

Larabee looked around to make sure they were not being overheard. "I've heard that you had a reputation as a square-shooter with the Central Pacific, McCabe. You didn't come here just to see steel bein' spiked down, and whoever took that shot at you doesn't seem to want you here."

Kirby waited, saying nothing. Larabee hesitated, then blurted it out. "There's somethin' off color with this railroad. There's all kinds of rumors among the crews out at the camps. If you can smoke out the trouble, I'm backin' you."

"Thanks," Kirby said. "I might need help and plenty of it."

"I'm just a railroad bull with two hard fists," Larabee said. "I'm hired to keep order in Antler an' in the camps and discourage freight thieves. But I like a good, straight track to run on."

Chapter 7

Kirby ate breakfast at dawn at a cafe and made his way to the railroad yards where a work train was preparing to pull out. In addition to a dozen flats, carrying steel rails, there were tie cars and commissary cars and two dilapidated wooden coaches which workmen were boarding.

Jem Larabee was waiting. He gave Kirby only a wink and a signal to board the train, but did not join him. Larabee took a seat at the far end of the coach.

The passengers were mainly tarriers from the steel and grading gangs en route back to the camps after spending their pay in Antler. Half a dozen blue-shirted cavalrymen, also red-eyed after sprees in town, sat together in the waist of the car, disdaining the railroad men and looking forward with no joy to returning to their lonely task of guarding Grand Pacific construction crews.

He discovered there were feminine passengers in the coach. Norah Logan was aboard with a middle-aged, plump woman companion. She had been seated before

Kirby arrived. Hovering over them was a nervous, white-collared railroad official.

Norah Logan turned with deliberation and looked at Kirby. Again there was a question in her eyes — and a challenge. She was asking herself what was taking him to the camps, and was preparing to meet whatever trouble he might bring.

She found no answer in Kirby's expression, and turned away. The presence of the daughter of the company president put the railroad workers and soldiers on their good behavior. They put aside their traditional feud and a strained armistice prevailed.

The car rocked along over the new roadbed. The country was treeless, with only scrub brush finding sparse foothold in the washes the track bridged on trestles. Presently, a low line of ragged bluffs began to glint on the horizon to the northwest. Squaw Buttes.

Kirby well remembered this region. He had spent the better part of a summer in this area with Ray Coleman's survey party. The Sioux and Cheyennes had not been exactly on the look for scalps that year, but would not have hesitated to have wiped out intruders if the sign had been right.

It was different now. The tribes had declared war, but the Bozeman Trail, far to the west, apparently was the storm center. Kirby had heard that the chain of forts the Army had established along the Bozeman were under virtual siege.

He singled out landmarks. Soldiering and railroading on the frontiers had schooled him in remembering the features of the trails and the terrain over which he had ridden. This route the Grand Pacific track followed had been mapped by Raymond Coleman as feasible from the Missouri River as far west as what was then known as Squaw River.

He sat recalling other things, past and present. The young buffalo he had downed with a long, chance shot at a time when they'd had nothing to eat except hardtack for two days. He remembered how delicious those hump ribs had tasted, spitted and braised black over a fire.

Norah Logan moved into his thoughts. As though this intruded on her mood, she turned involuntarily. Again their eyes met. Annoyed, she turned away and remained rigidly oblivious of him for the remainder of the journey.

Evidence of new, raw civilization began to appear. Brakemen hurried through the cars with brake clubs. The slowing train rumbled across a new trestle that spanned a sizable water course. Squaw River. Shiloh River, as Horace Logan had renamed it. Like the Missouri, it was carrying considerable water from the storms higher on the plains.

The train halted and Kirby alighted on a temporary plank platform alongside a track that was still being ballasted by gandy dancers. The new rails stretched westward from Shiloh River, straight as an arrow. A mile or more away he could see the activity and the dust where crews were laying rails. The tie crews were working another mile in advance of the steel gang.

End of steel! This was a camp on wheels, which soon would be moving on. A feverish clot of humanity. Bull teams and cook wagons. Cavalrymen and Pawnees. Blueshirted gang bosses and mule skinners.

Steel! More steel! That was the order of the day here.

Norah Logan and her companion were met by a big, square-jawed Irishman who had all the earmarks of a two-fisted construction boss. He came hurrying, lifting his battered hat, and led them toward his office car that was the nerve center of the job — the whipcracker's headquarters.

Jem Larabee joined Kirby. "That's Mike

Callahan," he said. "We'll find saddle horses ready for us at the company corral. I asked for them by telegraph this morning. I said it was an inspection trip by a company man."

A shrill note registered on Kirby's ears above the medley of sounds around him. It was an outcry he had heard in the past.

He whirled. One of the camp workmen, off duty for the moment, had walked away from the buildings into the open sagebrush. He had a rifle in his hands, and was shading his eyes, peering, evidently believing he had spotted game — an antelope perhaps.

The man had halted, having heard that same sound. He suddenly lifted his gun, fired at something, then turned and began racing desperately back toward camp.

But too late. Indians rose around him from the grass. It was over in the time it takes to draw a few deep breaths. The man died and was scalped as Kirby and the others stared, paralyzed.

None of the cavalry detail was near, being on duty mainly with the steel gang ahead. The Indians were Sioux, Kirby saw. They seemed to vanish into the earth again. Kirby made out the faint, saffron line of a dry wash that cut across the plain.

The yells of the Indians drifted back on the wind. They had taken a scalp within sight of two hundred men.

Howls of fury arose in the camp. Men dropped their tools and ran to seize up stacked rifles. They all began racing into the sagebrush — a scattered, disorganized mob, the majority of whom were unarmed or whose weapons were not loaded.

"Sure, an' 'twas Pat O'Toole, himself, the bloody divils murthured!" a man screeched as he ran past Kirby, brandishing an Enfield rifle that looked like it had seen service in the Civil War. "Come on, me boys. They're hidin' there in the grass. 'Tis a slow death we'll give the painted, treacherous —"

Kirby came to life. His voice was leathery and authoritative. "Company—y-y halt!"

That did it. The majority — and perhaps all of them — had fought in the war on one side or the other. Discipline had been ground into them. They halted to a man.

"About face, you fools!" Kirby roared. "You're running into an ambush!"

Sanity returned. They recognized him as an officer, and obeyed. By the time the cavalrymen arrived, they had withdrawn to the camp.

There were only two squads of troopers. Their lieutenant, a thin-faced, tired officer, apparently knew Indians and their ways.

He and his men recovered the body of Patrick O'Toole, whose native curiosity had lured him to his death. He sent scouts ahead. They were driven back, for they found Indians in force, hidden in the breaks of the plain.

The Sioux, their ambush failing, finally appeared in the open in the distance. It was a sizable party, more than forty warriors, Kirby estimated, and apparently well-armed. The Sioux were mounted now. They lined the crest of a swell out of rifleshot, jeering and daring the cavalry and the construction men to fight them.

The cavalry lieutenant refused that invitation. Some hot-heads among the railroad crews tried to taunt him into taking up the Sioux challenge.

"Go back to work," the cavalryman said. "That man was scalped because he refused to obey orders not to wander. If any more of you are anxious to do the same, I'm not stopping you. My job is to see that this cursed railroad gets built."

The Sioux finally vanished. The crews angrily settled back into their routine.

Kirby saw that Norah Logan was

standing on the steps of Callahan's office. She should have fled out of sight, by rights, but she had remained there and had seen the killing and the scalping.

As the blanket-covered body of Patrick O'Toole was carried past, she spoke to the stretcher bearers. "See to it that he's given burial in sacred ground, and that High Mass is sung. I'll pray for the repose of his soul, even though I may not be of his religion. If he leaves a wife or children, I am telling you they will never be left in want. The railroad will see to that. My father will see to it."

She was speaking for both the Grand Pacific and her father. Danger and violence and death were no strangers to the brawny men in the steel gang. The majority of them had seen comrades die on battlefields. But they had been talking gloomily among themselves. Patrick O'Toole's death had cast a pall over them.

Many of them had families and responsibilities. Norah Logan had understood that and had faced the real issue. Kirby saw their mood change. They began doffing their hats to her.

"We thank ye, indeed, ma'am," a spokesman said. " 'Tis two little ones an' a widow Pat O'Toole leaves in Antler."

122

"I'll call on them as soon as I get back to town tomorrow," Norah Logan said. "I'll see that they have anything they need."

Kirby knew she had solved a situation that might have cost the Grand Pacific many of its workers and set construction back.

"What is she doing here?" he asked Larabee.

"Came out to look out for arrangements for the shindig her father is putting on."

"Shindig?"

Larabee pointed toward a crew of men who were clearing and leveling a strip of ground in camp. "After the banquet is finished in town tomorrow night, they'll move the tent out here, for the general is bringing his whole herd of dudes, ladies an' all, to end of track on a special train. They'll be wined an' dined for three, four days while the men, such as are sober enough, try to shoot themselves a buffalo."

Kirby watched Patrick O'Toole's body being placed in a baggage car for the trip back to Antler. "Has this happened before?" he asked.

"A man on the grading gang up ahead was killed by an arrow a few days ago. Nobody saw the Indian who stretched the bowstring. There've been a couple of other scares. Young braves making fake rushes to try to stampede the men. A lot of yelling, but nobody hurt."

"That was no bunch of young braves this time," Kirby said. "They were full warriors. They were painted. I saw the feather of a chief among them. If I wasn't mistaken, it was Black Elk himself."

"You sort o' surprise me, McCabe. You don't mean to tell me you know Black Elk?"

"I smoked the pipe with him when I was with the cavalry. That was when I was with a detail guarding Raymond Coleman's survey party. Black Elk didn't like the thought of a railroad through his buffalo country even then, but Ray Coleman told him he was sure it would be built farther south. That was when Coleman was working for the Union Pacific, of course."

"I take it you're no longer of a mind to go on ahead to the grading camp?"

"Why not?"

"Lawdamighty, man! Didn't you see what just happened? It's twenty miles or more to the gradin' camp. The Indians might —"

Kirby grinned. "I learned back in the Ute country that a good, grain-fed horse, with a little swift in his legs, usually out-

124

runs an Indian pony and keeps a scalp in the right place. That's all I ask. A good horse."

"I reckon my hair's no more valuable than yours," Larabee sighed. "I'll danged well see to it that we ride the fastest horses Callahan's got in the string."

"Wait a minute! There's no call for you to go, my friend."

But Larabee was with him when they rode away from the steel camp a quarter of an hour later. The horses the wrangler cut to them from the stock in the railroad corral were sound roans that had seen enough work to toughen them.

Mike Callahan had also seen to it that they were heavily armed. They carried Henry repeating rifles in the boots and had braces of pistols strapped to their sides, along with a good supply of ammunition.

Looking back, Kirby saw that Norah Logan was watching their departure from a window in Callahan's office. She was no doubt puzzling over the purpose of Kirby's journey.

They passed the beehive of activity where the crews were pushing steel westward. Files of men ran with rails on their shoulders and other squads swung mallets, spiking steel to the ties that webbed the raw earth of the plains.

The same hectic pace was being set by the crews who were placing ties a mile ahead of the steel gang. This fell astern as they rode along the scar the grading crews had slashed in the plain. Graders usually worked a score of miles ahead. Kirby and Larabee were utterly alone.

The country here was broken and brushy with outcrops of worn buttes, veined by gullies. Except for the graded right-of-way, the country was as it had been since creation. Buffalo country. Indian country.

In spite of himself, Kirby felt tension rising. He was trying to watch every patch of brush, every dry wash. He had known this sensation before and it had only one name. Fear. He looked at Larabee and saw the same taut alertness in the older man. They grinned tightly.

"If somebody yelled right now, I'd jump right out'n my britches," Larabee admitted.

As though to mock him, a flock of sagehens broke almost at the feet of the horses with their customary thunder of wings. Both Kirby and Larabee had snatched rifles from the boots and were halfway out of the saddles to dive for cover

126

before they realized the truth. They resumed their places and laughed.

The roadbed entered a stretch of open buffalo grass where visibility was longer and they could relax a trifle.

Kirby often stood in the stirrups, sizing up the country. There was an increasing confirmation in his mind — a bitter acceptance of a theory that he had hoped against hope would prove to be wrong.

"And they say that Raymond Coleman really located this route," he finally spoke. "Is that correct?"

Larabee nodded. "That's right."

Kirby was moodily silent. Presently, the easy country gave way to broken terrain where deep coulees wound through a maze of wind-carved ledges. Expanses of muddy flats evidently had confronted the grading bosses with problems.

"Badlands of the Snowgoose River," Larabee said. "The graders had some grief here a couple of weeks ago. A flash flood wiped out a stretch of right-of-way, along with three or four fills and a couple o' trestles. They're still havin' some trouble findin' bottom in a couple of places ahead. It's throwed the work behind schedule. Costin' money too."

They came upon the grading crew that

was working at one of the trouble spots — the first sign of life in some ten miles. A detail of cavalrymen was standing guard over the score of workers who were handling wagons and teams and operating a steam pile driver, seeking to firm down a roadbed across a treacherous stretch of quicksand.

The sergeant in charge of the cavalry squad knew Larabee. He had been told by telegraph, which served the grading camps, about the scalping at Shiloh River.

"Ain't seen any sign of trouble here," he said. "Up to now. And I don't hanker to be jumped by that many Sioux. We're only eight soldiers. These tarriers will help in a fight, of course, but we'd be in trouble if we're jumped in force. I hear it was Black Elk leadin' that bunch on the Shiloh. That's bad medicine for sure."

When the cavalryman learned that Kirby and Larabee intended to continue ahead alone to the main grading camp, he eyed them morosely. "Better leave any gold an' diamonds an' rubies an' such-like here with me so I can send it to your kith an' kin. No use wastin' such trifles on a bunch of copper hides."

They thanked him and rode ahead. It was now late afternoon, but the grading

128

camp was only five miles away. The right-of-way carried them out of the breaks of the Snowgoose River and to the crest of a low divide.

The country ahead seemed even more broken than the past miles. To the north loomed the jagged ridges that were called Squaw Buttes.

Kirby halted his horse. "I've seen enough," he said. "We might as well go back and hang up for the night with the men at Snowgoose."

"Seen enough o' what?"

Kirby didn't answer that. "I've got a sudden yen to get back to Antler in time for Horace Logan's banquet," he said. "It might turn out to be quite a party."

"I've got a hunch you're not invited," Larabee said.

"I wouldn't miss it for anything. Not for, say — twenty-nine dead men."

Larabee studied him. "You've found out something on this ride."

"Could be."

"It's General Logan's hide you're after. Why? What's this about twenty-nine dead men?"

"Maybe you better invite yourself to the banquet, too," Kirby said.

"Maybe I will — if Black Elk an' his

playmates don't uninvite us on our way back to the Snowgoose."

However, they saw no sign of Indians on their return to the work camp, nor did they meet trouble the next morning on the ride back to the main camp at Shiloh River.

Kirby casually asked Mike Callahan if he had seen Raymond Coleman lately, but the camp boss said the locater hadn't visited the crews in some time.

He and Larabee climbed aboard the shuttle train that made the sundown run back to Antler. Norah Logan and her woman companion were in the coach. They were busy with paper and pencil, evidently listing supplies that would be needed for the entertainment of the dudes at the steel camp.

Norah Logan gave no indication she knew Kirby was aboard, but he guessed she had waited at the steel camp for his return in order to keep an eye on him. She could have caught an earlier shuttle train. She could, of course, have given orders the previous day to bar him from the camps, but she probably had decided to find out what he was up to. Larabee probably would be in for questioning.

Kirby tried to map his own course. He had in his hands the power to disgrace and ruin either Horace Logan or Ray Coleman. Or both.

For the Grand Pacific Railroad was being built into an expensive trap that would eat up millions of dollars and end in bankruptcy for the company.

Horace Logan evidently was engineering the swindle and was duping others into investing money in a company that was sure to fail. In either event, exposure would be a punishment worse than physical injury or even death for a man like Horace Logan. It would be the Logan name that would he trampled. The Logan pride.

But there was Raymond Coleman. Kirby was torn by conflicting tides. Ray had been almost a second father to him. On the face of it, Ray was hand-in-glove with Horace Logan, and the swindle was on a huge scale. It would be the stockholders who would lose, and among them, no doubt, would be hundreds of small investors.

There must be a mistake somewhere, some explanation for Ray's part in this scheme. It was impossible to picture him involved in fraud. He must find Ray and get the truth.

If Ray was to be found! Kirby suddenly had the hunch that this might be difficult. Impossible, perhaps. On the heels of that came a new, startling suspicion. He wondered if he had placed his finger on the real truth about Ray Coleman. If so, he knew now why the attempt had been made to murder him at Rolling Stone Manor.

He found himself gazing at Norah Logan. She had removed her bonnet and he could see only the warm richness of her hair above the back of the seat ahead. He drew a deeper breath. Any disgrace that came to Horace Logan would leave its mark on his daughter. And now, if Kirby's suspicion was borne out, the ugly word, murder, was involved in the pattern that had formed.

The train groaned to a stop at the Antler depot. Norah Logan was waiting for Kirby when he alighted from the coach. Her companion waited in the background. Norah Logan stepped into his path and spoke so that only he could hear.

"What are you up to?" she demanded.

Kirby was suddenly exhausted, sick to his soul of Antler and its ugliness and its deceits.

"Won't you ever give up?" she said huskily. "Shiloh is years in the past. Surely —"

She decided it was useless. She had only one more thing to say. "I'll tell you again that if you harm my father, I'll hound you to your grave."

She joined the plump woman and walked to a carriage that was waiting to take them to the Dakota House.

It was sundown. The Dakota House was already the focal point for the Eastern visitors who were awaiting the time to go to the tent where the banquet was to be held. Men in evening garb and women in finery were gathering. Jewels glittered, the trains of gowns were being held out of the mud.

Kirby shook hands with Jem Larabee. "Thanks," he said. "I hope I can ride the river with you again some time."

"Do you still aim to go to the banquet?"

Kirby didn't answer that for a time. "Yes," he finally said. "I've got to."

He left Larabee and walked to the Dakota House. He was in need of a shave and a bath. The visitors filled the hotel parlor and overflowed into the lobby. They were sipping champagne that waiters were bringing on trays.

Women drew their skirts aside and men glared disapprovingly as he made his way among them to the desk.

"Raymond Coleman, please," he said.

The clerk was curt and disapproving also as he informed Kirby that Mr. Coleman was out. No, Mr. Coleman had not occupied his room for several days.

When would Mr. Coleman be back? Now, how would he, the hotel clerk, know the plans of a busy man like Mr. Coleman? Would there be any message?

"No message," Kirby said.

He turned away. And found himself face-to-face with Horace Logan.

There was no recognition for a moment in the tall, elderly man's eyes. Then memory seemed to dawn. Horace Logan had been drillmaster for the raw contingent of Lockport recruits when they had first been mustered into service on the courthouse esplanade in their home town. Later on, Kirby had become only one of the faceless men in the ranks, but Horace Logan had not forgotten the days in Lockport.

He paused, his stern gaze inspecting Kirby closely. He had thinned some, and his beard had turned steel gray, but he still carried himself straight and erect. He was a distinguished figure in immaculate evening dress. It was plain that he was still in the habit of giving orders — and seeing them obeyed. As at Shiloh.

"Do I know you, young man?" Horace Logan demanded.

"You should," Kirby said. "You sentenced me to death along with twenty-nine other men. The name is McCabe. I take it you remember that name."

Horace Logan stood still straighter. "I do remember it," he said icily.

He had been accompanied by three or four of his Eastern visitors. They were waiting. He turned on his heel, joined them and moved away.

Kirby turned to leave the hotel. Reid Logan stood in his path. "It's been a long time since Omaha, McCabe, but I'm warning you that I'll hold you to answer for anything that might happen to the general."

"At least you Logans are of a single mind," Kirby said. "The same notice was served on me by your sister not many minutes ago."

Chapter 8

He left the Dakota House. But his problem had not been solved. There was no question now but that his failure to find Raymond Coleman was not a matter of chance. He was being avoided.

Twilight was coming. An orchestra began playing in the tent where the banquet was to be served. Kirby returned to the Buffalo Hotel where he shaved and bathed and donned laundered and pressed garb that he had left with the housekeeper.

He debated for a moment, then buckled on his own six-shooter. It was a more compact weapon than the Colt given to him by Stella Venters. It had a shorter barrel and was covered by the skirt of his coat. Even so, there was no disguising the bulge of its presence.

Darkness had come when he returned to Lincoln Street. The banquet was starting in the tent, for he could hear the rattle of tableware and the hum of conversation mingling with the strains of the orchestra.

He walked down the street to the Four Aces. Stella was dealing faro. The chairs

136

were filled at her table, but business at the other games was slack. Horace Logan's banquet evidently held the center of attention.

Again Stella saw him the instant he entered, as though she had been expecting him and hoping against hope he would not appear.

He had come here intending to speak to Stella alone and insist that she talk, insist that she tell him of what she was afraid.

She must have sensed this in him, for a desperate appeal was in her, a frantic plea that he would not try to force information from her.

Once more he could not bring himself to go ahead with the purpose. She saw that he had changed his mind and it was as though a weight had been lifted from her. Then, her expression froze. She was looking past him at the swing doors back of him by which he had entered.

He turned. There was nothing there. However, the bat-wing doors were still fluttering. Someone had started to enter, then had suddenly retreated.

Kirby walked out of the Four Aces. There were many persons in the block, but the only stroller near enough to have started to enter the casino was Barney

Inchman's bodyguard, the thin, black-clad Parson Slate.

There was no reason why a man could not change his mind at a casino doorway and decide to go elsewhere. But Kirby was certain that Slate had followed him, and had parted the doors of the Four Aces to make sure of his whereabouts.

At that moment the solid jar of an explosion rattled windows and doors in the Street. Kirby heard glass falling.

The blast had taken place down a side street at the Buffalo Hotel, where Kirby had taken quarters. He raced to the scene. Dust fogged the street and guests were still pouring from the structure. However, the major part of the building seemed undamaged. The explosion had occurred at the rear of the structure.

Kirby forced his way inside and mounted the stairs. Wreckage littered the rear of the hall. Men were peering into the room he had occupied. The door had been blown off. A portion of a wall was sagging.

"Poor feller!" an ashen-faced man was saying. "He never knowed what happened."

Blood and flesh spattered the wrecked room. The torn body of a man lay among the debris. Dust and fumes still drifted. A cloying, sweetish odor prevailed.

"What was it that blew up?" someone asked, appalled. "Thet don't smell like black powder."

Kirby supplied the answer. "Blasting oil," he said. "Nitroglycerin. The touchiest, trickiest stuff in the world to handle."

He had become familiar with that sickly odor during the building of the Central Pacific. Invention of practical ways to use nitroglycerin had been a big factor in blasting a right-of-way across the granite passes of the Sierra Nevada. It had speeded the task by months, perhaps years. But, in spite of all precautions, it had taken lives.

"What'd the fella want with that stuff in his room?" a man asked.

"It wasn't his room," Kirby said. "It was mine."

They stared. "Looks like somebody might have been tryin' to fix a deadfall for you, mister, an' got caught in his own trap," a man said nervously. "He might have killed us all," he added, aggrieved.

Kirby was suddenly sure he had the answer to why Parson Slate had been keeping tab on him. It had been Slate's job, no doubt, to make sure Kirby did not return to the hotel before the trap had been set.

Kirby salvaged what he could of his belongings. Except for dust and plaster stains, his personal effects had come through with little damage. His rifle only needed cleaning.

Jem Larabee arrived. He arched an eyebrow at Kirby. "It does seem like you're mighty unpopular with somebody. You've been lucky, up to now. But luck has a way of running out."

"I've been fretting over the same thought," Kirby said.

"Who would want to blow you sky high?"

"Seems like I wasn't the one who got blown," Kirby said. "Let me know when you find out who this fellow is — or was."

"I already know. His name was Pete Jennings. He worked for the G.P. Black powder shooter. Top man at blasting jobs when he was sober. But he'd steal his own mother's last cent for the price of a bottle when he got thirsty."

Larabee paused. "He must have got thirsty tonight an' needed a little money for a bottle."

"This time," Kirby said, "he dropped the bottle. He should have stayed with black powder. Nitro's nothing for a drunken man to handle."

"You figure he aimed to plant this so you'd knock it down when you came in?"

Kirby nodded. "Then it might have been set down as an accident."

"What do you aim to do now?" Larabee asked.

"The banquet," Kirby said. "Remember?"

"You mean you're still goin' there?"

"I didn't get dressed up in my best shirttail just to talk to a railroad badge toter like you."

Kirby brushed plaster dust from his hands, looked at his boots and sighed. "And I just shined 'em up."

He left his salvaged belongings with Titus Tinker for safe keeping and left the Buffalo Hotel alone. He walked down Lincoln Street to the Dakota House. From the tent on the adjoining showground came the voice of a speaker whose words were drawing occasional bursts of applause. The eating was finished. Horace Logan was well into his flowery speech.

Kirby halted abruptly and flattened against the face of the hotel in a dark area. In a moment, Parson Slate's thin figure loomed up. Kirby stepped in the man's path, bringing a collision that staggered his target.

He was dealing with a killer. Slate tried to draw, but Kirby had anticipated that. His fingers gripped the man's arm. He wrestled him violently around into a hammerlock position. Slate began to gasp with agony as his shoulder was in danger of being dislocated.

"The next time I catch you following me," Kirby said softly, "I'll bust that arm. It's your gun arm, isn't it?"

He released the man. Slate nursed his aching arm. "You fool!" the man breathed. "How long do you think you'll live — ?"

Slate broke off, reason overcoming his fury. He knew he had already said too much. Then he turned and walked away. Kirby stood gazing after him. He was thinking that Slate was Barney Inchman's man, not Horace Logan's. But only money talked with a person like Slate. He could have changed sides — for a price.

Kirby walked to the tent. The lights that glowed inside gave it the appearance of a big Halloween lantern. He paused in the entrance. A colorful audience sat at long tables set with linen and silver and adorned with flowers and the carved ice nymphs that Kirby's plainsman informant had scorned. The effigies were beginning to melt.

Horace Logan was on his feet at the speaker's table — a distinguished and aristocratic figure.

". . . and I tell you, ladies and gentlemen, that this is the mightiest project of all time. The Grand Pacific is destined to be the nation's lifeline, its artery that will pulse with the blood of the heart of America. The Union Pacific was a great achievement, but it was burdened by debt and political corruption. That will not be the case with the Grand Pacific."

He paused while applause came, then continued.

"We will open another vast, new country into which farmers and stock raisers will find free land. They will build a mighty empire on these plains and in the Oregon country. Does any man here doubt that we can do this thing?"

Kirby stepped into the lighted tent, drawing a deep breath to interrupt the speaker.

But the hard muzzle of a six-shooter was punched into his side. "No you don't, McCabe!"

The man with the gun was Reid Logan. He rammed the muzzle harder into Kirby. "March!" he ordered softly. "Out of here! The way you came in!"

"Go ahead and shoot," Kirby said. "Right in the back. The best target for a Logan."

He still intended to interrupt Horace Logan's speech. But a woman's hand was placed over his mouth. It was a slim hand, but with strength.

"No!" Norah Logan murmured fiercely. "Please don't try to talk. Don't shoot him, Reid."

Her lips were almost against Kirby's ear. "Don't make a scene here. Not until we talk this over. Come with us."

She had removed the six-shooter from his holster, disarming him. "I've got his gun, Reid," she whispered, her voice suddenly quavery. "He can't harm Father now."

She wore a dark evening gown, and a tiny, stylish opera cap adorned with seed pearls. A diamond pendant hung at her bosom and pearl earrings bobbed from her ears. She had long gloves.

"I didn't come here to shoot anybody," Kirby said. "Least of all, Horace Logan. All I intend to do is to tell these people how he's trying to swindle them."

"Swindle?" Reid Logan echoed. "What do you mean?"

"You know what I mean," Kirby said. "You people are out to fleece anybody who

144

invests in this crooked scheme. This railroad will be bankrupt inside of six months."

He looked closer at their faces. "Don't try to play innocent," he said jeeringly. "Don't tell me you don't know what your father is up to."

But there was a sudden uncertainty in him. They seemed thunderstruck. Genuinely so.

They were attracting attention. Heads were turning. Norah Logan gripped his arm. "We don't know what you're talking about, but this is not the place to discuss it."

She and her brother almost forcibly walked him out of the tent. Kirby found himself giving in to them in spite of himself.

Once they were outside, he halted. "Anything I have to say, I aim to say in there where everybody can hear it."

"Exactly what *are* you going to say?" Norah Logan demanded.

"I've already told you. I want to warn the lambs Horace Logan brought to the frontier that they're to be butchered by the wolves."

"How dare you!" she exclaimed. "My father never did a dishonest thing in his life."

"How about ordering thirty men to die so as to save his high and mighty pride?"

She was almost sobbing. "We've gone over this before. Isn't it time, Mr. McCabe, that you got over this terrible hatred of my father. Is that why you came here and cooked up this ridiculous charge of fraud against him?"

Kirby looked at Reid Logan. "She sounds sincere. A person would almost believe she doesn't know what's going on. But you're not that innocent, are you?"

"Just what do you say *is* going on?"

"The Grand Pacific is heading in the wrong direction west of Shiloh River," Kirby said. "It's building into rough country where it will go bankrupt trying to bridge marshes and quicksand rivers. It will have to deal with grades and curves that will run up operating costs no railroad can afford."

Norah Logan started to speak, but her brother motioned her to remain silent. "McCabe," he said, "you ought to have the decency to make such accusations face-to-face with my father."

"That's what I've been trying to do."

"You're wrong, but you could do damage that can't be repaired if you made wild statements in public. My father ought to have the chance to hear you privately and to deny this if you are wrong."

In the tent, a long burst of applause marked the end of Horace Logan's speech. The banquet was over. Kirby heard the stir and buzz of conversation as the guests arose to leave.

"It looks like I've lost my chance, right now at least," he said. "But I'd be only too happy to face Horace Logan and brand him for what he is. A swindler. And a murderer of soldiers. You name the time and place."

"The sooner the better," Norah Logan said grimly. "Reid, find Father and bring him to our rooms at the hotel. I'll wait for you there with this man."

"Not the hotel," her brother said. "There'd be no privacy there. Too many people are wanting to buttonhole Dad, and they'd crowd in. How about the parlor car? He'd have a better chance of slipping away to the car without attracting attention."

"Is it necessary to be *that* careful?" she protested.

Her brother looked at Kirby. "I'm afraid so. I think we're in for trouble."

She said to Kirby, "Is that satisfactory? If so, follow me."

"I'll follow you," Kirby said. "Incidentally, you have some property that belongs to me."

"Yes. Your gun. And I'll use it, if need be. I want to be very sure you understand that."

"I understand. But, there's a little matter that bothers me. We might have company."

"Company?"

"Someone keeps trying to look over my shoulder. Someone took a pot shot at me the other night. Ruined a good hat. Someone tried to blow me up at my hotel room tonight. Ruined a good room. Killed some fleas, maybe. And killed the man they sent to do the job."

Her breath caught. "I heard an explosion. So that was it? Who — ?"

She peered closer at him. "Are you trying to say you believe my father had anything to do with those things?"

"Who else would have a better reason to see me dead?" Kirby asked stonily. "Who else but myself knows about this crooked scheme?"

She looked around. They were in darkness, and she handed him his gun. "If anyone is following you, give them the slip," she said. "I can't go running around the railroad yards in a party dress. I'll stop by my room at the hotel and get something to wear over it. My father's special car is spotted on a siding on the far side of the railroad yards near the river. But you better meet me somewhere. There's a water tank just beyond the roundhouse. Wait for me at the tank. I won't be long."

"The railroad yards at night are no place for a woman, no matter what," Kirby said.

"I'm not afraid," she said.

She left him and walked toward the nearby Dakota House. Kirby strolled down Lincoln Street. He was trying to determine if he was being followed, but he could not be sure.

He suddenly faded between buildings, circled dark back areas at a fast pace, halting occasionally to listen. He was sure that he had shaken off anyone who might have been shadowing him.

He made his way to the railroad yards. The water tank Norah Logan had mentioned was easy to locate. As he neared it, she spoke from the darkness. She had wrapped a long, dark coat around her and was wearing a dark bonnet.

"I didn't expect to be here ahead of you," she said.

"I did some cross-tracking, in case somebody had a notion to follow me," Kirby explained.

149

She led the way across sidetracks. A varnished coach with a brass-trimmed observation platform stood alone on a spur that ended in a wooden barrier near the brushy lip of a bluff. Kirby could hear the rushing current of the muddy Missouri River sighing at the foot of the steep descent.

"Father's private car," she said. "We've got a suite at the hotel, but Father uses it sometimes to hide away when the pressure gets too great. He isn't as young as he used to be."

Kirby shivered a little. "I've seen more cheerful places for a powwow," he commented.

"You don't happen to be thinking that a body could be disposed of in the river tonight and nobody would be the wiser, now would you?" she asked blandly.

"The thought," Kirby said, "did occur to me."

He knew she was enjoying this little triumph she had finally achieved. He helped her up the steps of the car. It was locked but she had a key. They stepped into the dark interior. Kirby felt deep carpet underfoot, and smelled the richness of leather and velvet and linen.

Norah moved down the length of the car in the darkness drawing drapes, leaving them in utter darkness. He heard her fumbling around and presently she lighted one of the oil lamps in a cluster.

Horace Logan evidently used the car for sleeping at times, for there was a berth-type bed which could be curtained off. A pantry occupied the far end of the coach.

She removed her bonnet and started to toss it on the berth, but thought better of it and placed it on a sofa.

"So you've been told it's bad luck to put a hat on a bed," Kirby commented.

"I'm acquainted with all the superstitions," she said. "Including the ones about drowned men coming back to haunt their murderers."

Then she remembered Shiloh and knew that her attempt to taunt him had back-fired.

They remained silent, waiting. It was some time before they heard footsteps crunching in the cinders outside. Reid Logan's voice cautiously hailed the car, and his sister unlocked the door.

Instead of Horace Logan, his companion was a balding, fleshy, broad-jawed man in evening clothes, with shaggy, graying brows that hooded wise eyes.

"Why, Mr. Garrett?" Norah exclaimed.

Her brother closed and locked the door,

and spoke to Kirby. "This is Mr. Martin Garrett. He is vice-president of the Grand Pacific and is executive officer in charge of all construction work."

"How about Horace Logan?" Kirby demanded. "Where is he?"

Martin Garrett spoke. He had a harsh, peremptory manner. "The general is resting and can't be disturbed. He has been under great strain lately. The speech tonight was a little too much for him."

Norah uttered a gasp of alarm. "You mean he's ill?"

"Nothing to be worried about, I'm sure. He'll be all right tomorrow, my dear. Only a slight indisposition. The doctor says all he needs is a good night's rest."

"Doctor? A doctor was needed?"

"Only to give him something so he can sleep. He does not need further excitement tonight. That's an order. Your brother understands."

Kirby spoke caustically. "What he means is that the general doesn't want to see me tonight. Or any other night."

Garrett scowled. "Reid, is this the person you said had something important to say to your father?"

"I'm the man," Kirby said.

"If it's a personal matter it will have to

wait," Garrett said. "If it concerns the Grand Pacific, you can take it up with me."

"It's both," Kirby said.

"State it," Garrett snapped. "I'm busy tonight."

"I'll make it brief," Kirby said. "This railroad isn't ever going to get to Oregon. Over the present route, at least. Or even to the mountains. The only place it will go is into the hands of a receiver."

Martin Garrett glared. But Kirby felt that the man was not as surprised as he pretended.

Garrett wheeled on Reid Logan. "Did you know this was what this man had to say?" he thundered. "Thank the Lord, I intercepted you before you got to your father with this nonsense. It might have killed the general."

He turned on Kirby. "What sort of a scheme are you up to?"

"As construction chief," Kirby said, "you, of all persons, can't help but know that the country you're building into will ruin this railroad. And, surely, the president of the railroad, who brought these people here to prod them into throwing their money down a well, knows it too."

"You must be insane!" Garrett raged. "What did you say this fellow's name was, Reid?"

"Kirby McCabe," Reid answered. "He helped build the Central Pacific. I don't know what else he might be, but he isn't exactly crazy."

"Then it must be blackmail. He knows what a story like that might do to us now, no matter how false it is. What is it you want, McCabe? Money?"

"I only want to see Horace Logan and tell him in his teeth that he's not only a swindler but a murderer," Kirby said. "As for you, you know I'm telling the truth about the location of your railroad."

"Ridiculous! We had the best engineer in the business locate our right-of-way."

"Who?"

"Raymond Coleman, of course. If you were with the Central Pacific, as you claim, you know him and his reputation."

"I know Ray Coleman. He surveyed this territory a few years ago. He was hired by the Union Pacific to go over every possible alternate route than the one they used. There *is* a good location for a railroad west of here, but it's not the one you're following beyond Squaw River. Shiloh River, you call it now. Coleman definitely labeled that path as impractical. But he did map a route north of Squaw Buttes over which a railroad could be built, when the time came."

Garrett uttered a snort of derision. "Rubbish."

"You don't want the truth, do you?" Kirby said. "I know Raymond Coleman too well to believe he'd be a party to what's going on. You're lying when you use his name. Ray Coleman is in South America."

"On the contrary, he's here," Garrett said. "Here in Antler. And now what do you say?"

"I'd like to talk to him," Kirby said. "Take me to him."

"You mean you still persist in accusing a man of Mr. Coleman's reputation?" Garrett demanded. "We have letters praising his ability and recommending him from such people as Dr. Durant of the Union Pacific and Leland Stanford and Collis P. Huntington of the Central Pacific."

He turned to Reid Logan. "Find Mr. Coleman and ask him if he can spare us a few minutes, Logan, please."

"Where will I find him?" Reid asked.

"At the Dakota House, most likely. Or ask someone. He ought to be easy to find."

"Are you sure he's in town?" Kirby demanded.

"Naturally. I personally asked him to be present at the banquet tonight to help answer any questions that might be asked."

155

"You saw him there?"

Garrett frowned impatiently. "It was impossible to see every face, of course. But he certainly must have been there."

Kirby was suddenly sure that Garrett was lying. The man was only stalling for time. He turned to Reid Logan. "Don't waste your time looking for Ray Coleman. You won't find him and this man knows it. Coleman hasn't been seen for days. At least he hasn't occupied his room. I inquired at the Dakota House today."

Garrett uttered a snort. "Then he must have been called out to the camps for some reason. Reid, send a message to Mike Callahan to find him and —"

"That's no use either," Kirby said, certain now that Garrett was trying only to delude Reid and Norah Logan. "Ray Coleman isn't out there. And hasn't been for days."

"How do you know that?"

"Callahan told me that at Shiloh River."

"What were you doing at Shiloh River?" Garrett demanded.

"Making sure I was right about the high blaze you people are running," Kirby said.

Garrett whirled to leave. "I can't waste time talking to this man, Reid. The best thing to do is send for Jem Larabee and have him locked up or run out of Antler before he causes real trouble."

"That," Kirby said, "might take some doing. I don't run easy. Or scared."

Reid Logan spoke. "Give us a few days, McCabe. Time to look into this thing."

"What?" Garrett exploded. "You don't mean you're putting any stock in this fellow's story?"

Reid Logan ignored that. "What do you say, McCabe? This is no time for anyone to cast doubts on the company's prospects. It might cause a panic. A lot of people might get badly hurt financially."

"But not the Logans," Kirby said.

"Why not the Logans? We'll be hurt most of all."

"Do you really expect me to believe you don't know you're bankrupting this company and that you didn't bring those people by the trainload, so you could pick their pockets."

He pushed past them and left the car.

"Wait!" Norah's voice called after him. She descended from the car and came hurrying to overtake him in the darkness.

"I want to talk to you," she said. She had lowered her voice so that Garrett and her brother could not hear, for they had emerged on the platform of the parlor car and were peering curiously.

"Go ahead and talk," Kirby said.

"Not here," she whispered.

"I can't imagine that there's anything we've got to say to each other," Kirby said.

"I might have something to say about Raymond Coleman that might interest you," she replied.

Kirby tried to study her in the faint light. "Now you *do* interest me," he said.

"Where can we meet in, say half an hour?" She anticipated his refusal. "Don't be a fool! I'm not setting a trap for you."

"How about the Dakota House?" he said.

"No. There are too many people who might see you there. What about the place you're staying. I can slip out of the Dakota House and come there."

Kirby rolled it over in his mind, then nodded. "All right. The Buffalo Hotel. It's on Fifth Street."

He left the railroad yards. A carriage passed him on Lincoln Street, carrying two occupants. One was Horace Logan, decked out in a gaudy, fringed, white elkskin coat and a big white sombrero. He was smiling and waving to acquaintances on the sidewalk.

Horace Logan appeared to be in the best

158

of health and spirits. So the story about his being indisposed had been a fabrication also. Horace Logan evidently had not wanted to face Kirby and had sent Martin Garrett as a buffer.

Chapter 9

Kirby returned to the Buffalo Hotel. For one thing, he wanted walls around him and a door that he could lock. He saw no indication that he was being followed, but he believed that his trail would soon be picked up again.

A few sightseers were still inspecting the wreckage, but the edge of interest had worn off. Pete Jennings' mangled body had been taken away and the damaged area of the structure was roped off. Fallen plaster had been cleared away.

Titus Tinker was still moaning his misfortune when Kirby appeared at the booking desk. He was a round, moon-faced man in a collarless white shirt. He was something less than pleased by Kirby's return. He was even less enthused when he learned that Kirby was still in need of shelter for the night.

"Ain't it enough that you got one corner blowed off my place," he lamented. "An' half my tenants movin' out an' askin' for their money back."

Kirby pointed out that this created va-

160

cancies that brought no income, and that, inasmuch as he was entitled to a refund also, it would be of mutual benefit to both if he occupied one of the undamaged vacancies.

"It isn't likely anybody will try to blow me up a second time," he argued. "At least tonight."

Titus Tinker sighed and handed him a key. "Room 210," he said. "Best in the house. Keep your door locked this time."

"It was locked," Kirby said. "Your doors are too easy to open, my friend."

He suspected that Tinker had been bribed into permitting Pete Jennings to enter his room. If so, the explosion must have been an unpleasant reward for the hotel owner.

Tinker handed over the belongings Kirby had salvaged. He ascended the stairs and found the room that had been assigned to him. It had escaped damage. He drew the curtains, then lighted the lamp and locked the door.

He rolled a cigarette and waited. He tried to tell himself that he must be going out of his mind to think of keeping this appointment. The chances were, he argued with himself, Norah Logan was only acting as bait to immobilize him while her father could act to meet the threat he was offering to their scheme. Indeed, he might be sitting in the trap he had first suspected, despite her vehement denial.

Still, he waited. He could not fully convince himself that she was aware of the swindle that was being perpetrated. On the other hand, there was the saying that blood was thicker than water. He kept remembering the night in Omaha when he had partly deflected Parson Slate's aim at Horace Logan's back. What he was recalling was Norah Logan's grief when she believed her father was dying. She loved her parent, believed in him. She might be so loyal she would shield him with every weapon at her command.

Footsteps approached his door. A hand rapped on the panel. Titus Tinker's voice spoke. "McCabe, are you in there? I've got a lady here what says she wants to see you."

Kirby had his six-shooter in his hand when he opened the door. But only Norah Logan stood in the hall with Tinker.

"I want to talk to Mr. McCabe alone," she said, and placed a coin in Tinker's hand.

"Well," Tinker said greedily. " 'Tain't regular."

"If it's more money you're after," Kirby said, "you're not going to get it. Run along now. And I have a habit of biting off the ears of anyone I catch eavesdropping on me. Keep that in mind, my fat friend."

He motioned Norah to enter the room and closed the door in Titus Tinker's face.

"My, my!" she remarked. "Isn't he the upright person, now."

She removed the coat and bonnet and sighed with satisfaction. "On such a hot night, the things a lady will do to protect her reputation."

"Titus Tinker will look out for your reputation," Kirby said. "He isn't far away. He probably is even risking an ear trying to listen in."

"Then we better keep our voices down," she said.

She was still wearing the evening gown. She had abandoned the satin cap and long gloves, but the pendant glittered at her bosom, and removal of the bonnet had revealed the pearl earrings still in place.

She saw Kirby's brows lift. "I feel sort of like a lost circus horse," she said. "I didn't want to go to my room and change. I stayed at the parlor car and came directly here."

She was trying to be casual about it, but

he could see that she was trembling. He pulled the only chair in the room around for her, and motioned her to accept it.

She smiled wanly. "Thank you. This has been rather a trying day."

"And it's going to be no ordinary night, from the looks," Kirby said.

"I came here about my father," she said. "And only about my father."

"Is that why your brother didn't come with you?"

"Reid is tied up with some important visitors. And I wanted to see you alone, as I told you."

"Well, we're alone."

"You're only trying to humiliate me," she exclaimed.

"And are you humiliated?"

"Infuriated is a better word. You try to put the wrong construction on everything we Logans do. Let me make it clear, Mr. McCabe, that I came here only because it was time two stubborn men — knuckleheaded would be more to the point — were made to understand each other."

"Namely?"

"You know the names. You and my father. He's accused you of being a turncoat and a coward. You are about to shout to the world that he's a cheat and a swindler."

"You're setting your sights too low," Kirby said. "I'd call him a full-scale confidence man. He's not dealing in small change. He's out to rook people of millions."

He added, "By the way, he made a quick recovery from his indisposition. I saw him riding in a carriage and in the best of health tonight after I left you and your double-tongued Mr. Garrett."

She shrugged. "I saw him also, but had no chance to talk to him. I suppose Mr. Garrett was only acting in what he thought was my father's best interests in keeping you apart."

She paused for a moment. "There's one item that is not clear in my mind. Just how is my poor father going to profit from this swindle that you talk about?"

"*Poor* father?" Kirby echoed, scornfully eying her jewelry.

"They're imitation stones," she said sweetly. "The diamond is paste. The pearls are not worth much. The real ones, which were family heirlooms, were put up as collateral for loans to my father in connection with promoting the Grand Pacific."

She continued to try to wither him with a superior smile. She ran her hands over her gown. "However, this dress is genuine.

165

It was my mother's wedding dress. I've altered it. Pretty, isn't it? But it didn't cost my father a penny."

She leaned forward. "If Grand Pacific goes down, the Logans go down with it. Every penny we have in the world is tied up in the railroad. Our home in Lockport is mortgaged, all the family silver and jewels have been sold or put up as security for loans. Everything. Everything we possess."

She leaned back. "Now tell me how we would benefit by this swindle?"

"You have a point there," Kirby admitted. "My only guess is that he intends to pull out with what he can milk out of these dudes he's brought here. And that will be considerable."

"Ridiculous. These people aren't fools. If they sense anything wrong, they'll go back East with the story. That will be the end of the Grand Pacific."

"And so you came here to throw your weeping form on my chest and ask me to keep quiet about your erring father?"

Her anger blazed but she got control of it. "Let's forget personalities and go over this matter practically."

"Practically? That means I'm to believe your father is a sincere, honest person who

166

makes a mistake now and then. Like the one at Shiloh. He came out of that as a general. His reward for a small error."

"Just what sort of a man is Mr. Coleman?" she asked abruptly.

"I'd always found him to be a square shooter," he said.

"I mean his physical appearance. What did he look like?"

Kirby frowned. "You ought to know. He was there in the Four Aces in Omaha the night your father was shot. He was sitting with me. He hasn't changed much, if any."

"I was too excited, too worried about my father to know who was in the place. Tell me what kind of a man he is. Tall? Short? Old? Young?"

She was touching on his own theory. A pulse began to throb in him. "You mean you really don't know what he looks like?" he asked. "Surely, you must have seen Ray Coleman since then, if he was doing such important work for your father as locating this railroad?"

"Yes, but only once. And that was a few days ago, here in Antler, right after I arrived with Reid. My father presented me to some of his business associates when I surprised him by walking into his office. One of them was introduced as Raymond Coleman."

167

"*Introduced* as Coleman?"

They peered at each other. "Apparently we have the same thought in mind," she said.

"Ray Coleman is about forty-five years old," Kirby said. "Five feet eleven, wiry and tanned. Blue-gray eyes, hair on the sandy hue and bald at the top. Quite intelligent. Quiet, easygoing."

He eyed her. "Does that mean anything to you?"

She made a wry grimace. "A lot of men could answer that description. He was not exactly a person who impressed me. I didn't like that long, pointed mustache. It looked artificial." She paused, then asked, "Your Mr. Coleman did have such a mustache? Or did he?"

"A regular six-inch spike," Kirby said. "He was proud of it."

"Oh dear!" she sighed. "That spoils everything. I thought I had been so clever."

"You mean you suspected the man was not the real Ray Coleman, but an imposter?"

"That thought had occurred to me," she admitted dolefully.

"As a matter of fact," Kirby said, "your thought was correct. This man *is* a fake. He isn't Ray Coleman."

She stared, her eyes wide. "Now why — how — ?"

"Ray Coleman used to have such a mustache," Kirby said. "It was his only vanity. And his trademark. But not for nearly a year. He got badly burned in a construction camp. Boiling tar. Some fool tried to put out a fire under a big tar pot with water, and the water hit the tar instead. Ray nearly lost his sight, but they saved his eyes. However, he had a scar on his upper lip they could do nothing with. He never could even sprout a mustache that would hide it."

He looked at her. "I guess they didn't know that Ray no longer had that fancy mustache — and never could have one again."

She was so excited she sank down again in the chair. "I *was* right. The letters from Dr. Durant and Mr. Stanford must have been forged. And the location he recommended for the railroad —"

Kirby halted her. "It won't work."

She subsided. "What won't work?"

"I might swallow the story that you never saw the real Ray Coleman personally. But your father hasn't any such excuse."

"I see," she said slowly. "You think I

came here with a cooked-up scheme to try to make it appear that my father is only the victim of some kind of a frameup."

"It wouldn't be the first time he's wriggled out over the bodies of dead men."

"Dead men?"

"Me, for one. They knew I was personally acquainted with Ray Coleman and would upset their scheme. The fake Coleman keeps out of sight as much as possible. I might be the only person around who was acquainted well enough with Ray Coleman to know the other was an imposter if I laid eyes on him. So they kept him out of my way while they tried to get rid of me. They —"

He broke off, struck by a new realization. "No! I wasn't the only one! Lee Venters!"

"Venters? The gambler? Isn't he the man who owned the gambling house in Omaha where my father was shot?"

"Lee Venters owned the same place here," Kirby said. "He was killed not long ago. Murdered. Here in Antler. It was set up to look like an accident."

He looked at her. "It was no accident. His wife is running the Four Aces here. They have a daughter. A beautiful girl of —"

He smashed a fist into a palm. "Timmy!

Of course! That's it! That's why Stella wouldn't talk. She knows the real Ray Coleman. And so does Timmy. My God! Maybe they're after them right now. They know the cat's about out of the bag. They're in too deep to back out now. They might try to silence everybody who knows the real Ray Coleman until they can cover up."

He seized up his gunbelt which he had hung on the frame of the bed and opened the door. He raced, hatless, for the stairs. He found that Norah was at his heels.

"Where are you going?" she panted.

"Go back!" he commanded.

There was a rear door in the lower hall and he left by that route. He raced through dark areas, circling sheds and stables, heading for the Venters' home on wheels.

"Wait for me!" Norah Logan gasped. She was following him, holding her skirts to her knees and running lithely.

He slowed. Not because he was waiting for her, but because Rolling Stone Manor showed against the stars ahead.

"What in the world . . . ?" she began as she joined him. That was all she could say, for Kirby clapped his hand over her mouth. Her question ended in a gurgle.

Lamplight showed in the windows of

Rolling Stone Manor. But the wheeled house was silent. Too silent. Kirby scanned the weedy flat. It was here that a killer had waited in ambush for him. So recently — and yet it seemed long ago.

Norah, sensing the deadly tension in him, remained motionless. Shadows moved. A distance away brush crackled. Men were there — running. Kirby had his six-shooter in his hand, cocked, but he did not fire.

He ran toward the house. "Stay back!" he warned Norah over his shoulder. "Stay back I say!"

She again refused to obey and followed him.

"Stella!" Kirby called. "Timmy!"

He heard muffled sounds as though someone was trying to scream. "Timmy!" Kirby shouted again. "It's Kirby McCabe!"

It was Stella's voice that answered. She was hoarse, hysterical. "They've taken her away! They've kidnaped Timmy."

He tore open the door of the house. Stella had been gagged and bound to a chair, but she had managed to work a hand loose and remove the gag.

"Take care of her!" Kirby said to Norah Logan.

He raced in pursuit of the running footsteps. A gun opened up ahead of him. Bullets raked the weeds around him. Someone was shooting wild, hoping to down him by chance.

He did not dare fire back, for fear of hitting Timmy. The gun ahead went silent. He could still hear running feet. His quarry had parted, taking opposite directions.

He heard a muffled sound and stumbled over Timmy, who lay in the weeds, struggling to free herself from a blanket that had been lashed around her. She, too, had been gagged.

Kirby knelt beside her, listening. But the abductors had dropped their burden and escaped. He freed Timmy. She choked and retched for a time, then began to weep. He lifted her and carried her toward the wheeled house.

She fought off the tears and said huskily, "I can walk, Kirby. Put me down. It'll only frighten Mother that much more, if she thinks I've been hurt."

Norah admitted them to the house. Stella, her hair fallen, her blouse torn and a bruise on her throat, came tearfully to take Timmy in her arms.

Kirby started to ask a question, but Norah motioned him to wait. "Give them a chance to get hold of themselves," she said.

"I'm all right," Stella said shakily. "Thank Heaven, you came, Kirby."

"How many of them were there?"

"Two, I believe, was all. They had gunny-sacks over their heads with eyeholes. They were in the kitchen before I knew we were in danger. I foolishly had neglected to lock the door. I guess they'd been waiting a chance like that. They threw a blanket over my head and choked me before I could make a move."

"Did you see them, Timmy?" Kirby asked.

"No more than a glimpse." She shuddered. "They looked like monsters. Those bags over their heads. I was never so scared in my life. I thought they'd killed Mother. I must have fainted. The next thing I knew, I was being carried over the shoulder of one of them. I thought I was smothering. I couldn't breathe. Then there was gunfire and they dropped me on the ground."

She added with a wan smile, "The one who was carrying me didn't seem to be too strong a man. I could hear him wheezing and puffing. I'm not exactly a child any more."

Norah put an arm around her. "Why would anyone try to harm you?"

174

She looked at Kirby and Stella, aware of a sudden silence. "I believe I know the answer to that," she said slowly.

Kirby spoke to Stella. "This is why you wouldn't talk to me, isn't it Stella? You were afraid something like this would happen. They *did* threaten you?"

"I found a note under the door one night," she said. "It was after Lee was killed. The day after. It said that if I kept my mouth shut about being acquainted with a certain person, Timmy might be allowed to grow up to be a beautiful woman."

She drew a deep breath. "That was all it said. That was enough. I knew then that Lee had been murdered and that they meant what they said."

She choked up. "They're vicious. Killers. They murdered Lee. They're trying to murder you. They'll keep on until they do. I heard about the explosion at the Buffalo Hotel."

She added desperately, "What can we do? I've been afraid to try to leave Antler. I know they've been watching me. Day and night. Where can we go? Where can we hide?"

Kirby looked at Norah Logan. "You tell her."

Norah's chin lifted. She understood. "What he means is that he's accusing my father of being back of what is happening here in Antler."

"Who else but your father?" Stella said bitterly. "He's Grand Pacific, isn't he? He hired a man he claimed was Raymond Coleman to locate the route. Lee and Timmy and I knew the real Ray Coleman. We had been friends from the days in Denver and Omaha. We were unlucky enough to know your father's man was an imposter. A fraud."

Norah Logan did not wither or flinch. "My father doesn't know the man is a fake," she said.

She saw the incredulity in Kirby's face. "As I remember it, Father met this man in Washington, D.C., only about a year ago. We were living there at the time while Father negotiated approval by Congress of the charter, and was busy with financial affairs. Father brought this man to our house for supper one night."

"How about Omaha?" Kirby demanded. "How about the Union Pacific? Ray Coleman had a big hand in —"

He broke off suddenly recalling a statement Ray Coleman had made that night in Omaha. Coleman had said that he had

176

never met Horace Logan personally, and that he knew the general only by sight. In that case it was quite possible that Horace Logan did not even know Coleman by sight.

"My father had no occasion to meet Raymond Coleman in those days," Norah explained. "He was interested only in the financial end of the Union Pacific. Mr. Coleman was a locater. As for the night Father was shot, men about to fight a gun duel usually don't waste time checking over the bystanders."

Chapter 10

Kirby tried not to believe Norah Logan. Again that didn't work. "You ought to be dealing a shell game," he said angrily. "That's what this thing is turning out to be. Guess under which shell is the man back of this."

He added, "If this is so, who brought the fake Raymond Coleman to your father in the first place?"

"I don't know," she said. "It is one point I failed to ask him about."

"Maybe you knew he wouldn't tell you."

She stamped her foot. "You *are* an aggravating man," she said. "I've told you that every penny we have in the world is at stake in this thing. Again I ask you, in the name of Heaven, why would my father be deliberately trying to bankrupt the Grand Pacific when it meant his own ruin too?"

"There are such things as milking a company — and the stockholders dry, then getting out of the country," Kirby said.

"And you really think my father is capable of anything like that?"

"He's done worse," Kirby said.

He thought for an instant she was going to slap him. She knew what he meant. The twenty-nine who slept at Shiloh. She fought for calmness. And won.

"Is it too late?" she finally asked.

"For what?"

"To change the location of the railroad if the one they're using is as wrong as you say?"

Kirby thought it over for a space. "No. Far from it. There'd be some loss, of course. They'd have to write off all grading west of Shiloh River, along with some bridges. They could salvage material. It wouldn't be much of a trick to pull back and build this side of the river, then swing west, north of Squaw Buttes. Raymond Coleman mapped that route as feasible."

"Again I'm going to ask you to wait before you do anything, and give us time to look into this."

"To give your father a chance to take to his heels with what he can steal before they come after him with a rope? Is that it?"

She was tight-lipped. "Even if you are right — and I'm not saying you are — it would ruin the Grand Pacific if this came out right now. It would cause a panic."

"It also might save a lot of money for people who are being prodded into buying

179

stock," Kirby said.

"On the contrary it would hurt people who've already put money into stock. The truth is that the company is skating on thin ice, financially. It must raise more money at once. My father's idea in bringing those wealthy people here from the East is his only hope of keeping construction going."

She gazed wrathily at his skeptical expression. "You make it all sound like dishonesty. Selling stock is the only way a job like this can be financed. If the Grand Pacific is built, it will make money. So what's wrong with selling stock in it? It will be a big benefit to those who buy it."

She paused. "What do you want me to do? Get down on my knees and beg. I'll do it, if that's what you'd like. Not for my father, but for the sake of people who've already invested money in the railroad."

She really started to go to her knees. It was not in humility, of course. It was only to heap coals of fire on his head.

He seized her and refused to let her humble herself. "You'd do anything, wouldn't you?" he raged. "Anything?"

"All I ask is a few days' time," she said. "Surely, you're not that vengeful?"

She had defeated him. "I'll think it over," he said.

180

She drew a long breath. She knew she had won. "Thank you," she said.

"I've got a feeling," Kirby said, "that I'm being sent out again by a Logan to be shot down while the Logans get out of a trap. You talk, but you don't explain anything. Who'd want to palm himself off as Raymond Coleman, just to ruin a railroad? Tell me that?"

"I've already told you that my father is fighting off receivership. You know what that means. The Grand Pacific already owns railroads as far east as Illinois. They're worth several million dollars alone. Then there are steamboats, barges and rolling stock and material already contracted for. Those things are worth a lot more money. In a receivership, they could be picked up for a song and that person, or persons would be in a position to build and own the road all the way to Oregon."

She looked at Kirby squarely. "The person back of this is so clever my father has never suspected anything underhanded was going on."

"Such as Barney Inchman?" Kirby asked.

"He's got a finger in it, no doubt," she replied. "I know that my father is worried about Inchman being here in Antler. But it must be more than Inchman. This is too

181

big for him. Important money is backing him."

"Just what do you intend to do next?" Kirby asked. "I want to make one thing clear. I'm going to keep track of your father. If he tries to leave Dakota, I'll stop him."

"That's your privilege," she said. "First, we'll investigate your claim about the location of the railroad. Reid is going to Shiloh River tomorrow with the excursion party. He can travel saddleback from there to look at the country."

"I'd advise him to take a troop of cavalry with him," Kirby said. "Even a Logan isn't bulletproof. Or arrowproof."

"You took that chance. And without cavalry."

"And my knees rattled all the way out and back. About all that kept me going was what Jem Larabee told me about the junket the Grand Pacific is putting on at the steel camp for the dudes. I wouldn't want to miss sampling some of that fancy grub the Grand Pacific is bringing in. In fact I might be the life of the party."

"Or the death of it. But what about Mrs. Venters and Timmy?"

"What do you mean?" Stella asked.

"You and Timmy will go along with us

on the train with the dudes," Kirby said.

Stella started to refuse, but Kirby added, "I can't leave you alone here in Antler. Let's not fool ourselves. There's too much money at stake for these people to be squeamish about another life or two — or even half a dozen. You and Timmy will be safer on the trip, where I can keep an eye on you."

"You may be right," Stella said with a sigh.

"I'll have you and Timmy stay with me at the Dakota House tonight," Norah said. "You will use my brother's room. He can put up somewhere else. Our rooms are adjoining."

Stella turned to Kirby for advice. He nodded. "You'll be comfortable there."

They all knew what he really meant. He believed they would be safer.

Norah gave him a slanting look. "Thank you," she said dryly. "Thank you again."

"For what?"

"For absolving the Logans of terrorizing Mrs. Venters and her daughter, at least, even though you're not so sure about other things."

She was right, of course. If her father was not back of the threat that had silenced Stella, the odds were that she had told the truth when she had said that he was the victim, rather than the originator, of the attempt to bankrupt the Grand Pacific.

He and Norah waited until Stella and Timmy selected what belongings they would need. He continued to puzzle over it as he puffed on a cigarette.

Parson Slate had been Inchman's man back in Omaha and was still his trouble shooter, no doubt. Kirby no longer entertained the belief that it had been Horace Logan's money that had hired men to try to kill him.

But, as Norah had said, there must be more to it than Inchman. "Who's the man your father believes in, the one he trusts completely?" he suddenly asked Norah.

She stiffened. "My brother. Are you trying to accuse him of this?"

"Perhaps."

"He's the one person in the world my father has complete faith in. He loves Reid. Oh, he would do anything for me, too. He loves me also. But Reid is his life. When Reid lost his arm at — at —" Her voice stumbled.

"At Shiloh," Kirby said harshly. "Don't be afraid to say that terrible word. He lost his arm there. And held me to blame."

184

She fought back tears. "Who are you to know how it was with Reid? You've never lost an arm, never faced the sympathy, the pity of people. He lay at death's door for weeks. He wanted to die. After he came home, he learned that my father blamed a soldier named Kirby McCabe for having brought the Confederate guns down on them. You were only a name to him then."

Emotion was shaking her. "I love my father, but I know his faults, his pride. He is a headstrong man who doesn't like to admit mistakes. He was sure you were to blame. Reid believed him."

Kirby listened to footsteps outside. A man's voice spoke. "Stella! Are you there, ma'am?"

Kirby's six-shooter was in his hand. Stella pushed it down. "That's Ben Carhart, my assistant at the Aces," she said.

Kirby opened the door and stood aside, the pistol ready, until Stella made doubly sure of the caller's identity. Ben Carhart was a tall, dark-eyed, black-haired man of forty with a clipped mustache and sideburns.

"There's trouble comin' at the Aces, Stella," Carhart said. "Maybe you better come an' take a look."

Kirby drew the man into the lighted room and closed the door. "What kind of trouble?" he asked.

Carhart eyed Kirby carefully. "Do I know you?"

Stella spoke. "Ben, this is Kirby McCabe. An old friend of Lee's, and a border cavalryman. You can trust him." She turned to Kirby. "And you can trust Ben to the limit."

Carhart grinned. "Thank you kindly, Stella. I heard Lee speak of Kirby McCabe. Spoke well of him. As for this trouble, I ain't sure just what brand of devilment it really is. I got a feelin' somebody's bein' set up to be cross-fired."

"Why do you say that?" Kirby asked.

"It's somethin' in the air. Maybe in my bones. There are strangers in the Aces. Fish eyes, for sure. Cold clams. The kind that show up where there's a killin' in the wind."

"How many?"

"Four, maybe five," Carhart said. "People drift in. Drift out. I can't always pick out the real slingers from the would-bes. But these cusses have got the earmarks of the genuine article. Fact is, I know one of 'em from the days on the Union Pacific. He was bad medicine then,

186

an' I don't reckon he's reformed none."

"Are they hanging together?"

"No. That's why I smell a cross-fire. Some innocent bystander is likely to have his brains blowed out by a stray slug."

"How're they working it?" Kirby asked. "Wait. Let me tell you. Loud talk. Ugly talk. Pretend they're drinking too much. And they all act like they're strangers to each other."

"I can see that you've been around considerable," Carhart said. "It'll start when the real target gets in the line of fire. That way, nobody will know who really fired the shot, an' it would be put down as an accident."

"They have a habit of causing accidents," Kirby commented. "Fatal ones. Anybody else that we know happen to be present at the Aces?"

"About the usual trade, except for these roughs."

"Is Parson Slate there? You know him, of course?"

"I know him. If he's there, I didn't see him."

"Barney Inchman?"

"No. Man, you ain't standing there, tryin' to say that Inchman — ?"

"I'm not trying to say anything," Kirby

said. He regretted having mentioned Inchman's name. If Inchman really was arranging a cross-fire, he would certainly not be present. Nor would Parson Slate. They would be very sure to have alibis.

The question was, if such a trap was being set, who was the intended victim.

Stella spoke. "They're still after you, Kirby." Her mind had raced along the same path as his thoughts. She came to him and said huskily, "Kirby, Kirby! Get out of Antler before they kill you. Like they killed Lee. It was no accident. I knew it from the start. He was hit with a horseshoe nailed to a club, so as to make it look like a horse had kicked him. Timmy and I aren't the only ones who aren't safe. They want you dead, above all."

"Maybe so," Kirby said. "But why would they be expecting me to go to the Four Aces? I had no idea of going there."

"They must know that you came here," Stella said. "They probably believe you'll go to the Aces with me."

Kirby mulled it over. "No. I can't agree with you. Whatever is going on at the Aces could hardly have anything to do with me."

He looked at Timmy's worried young face and chucked her under the chin. "Perk up. We're steering clear of any

188

deadfalls. Nobody is going to get hurt, least of all you."

"I'm not afraid," Timmy said. "Not for myself."

"Anyway, I'll find Jem Larabee and see that he camps in the shadow of you and your mother until all this business is straightened out. I'm sure Larabee can be trusted."

He turned to Carhart. "I'd appreciate it if you'd follow us. Sort of a rear guard. I'm sure you know how to cover a retreat. You've got the marks of a man who has soldiered."

"I handled heavier pieces durin' the war," Carhart explained, "but I assure you I'm not entirely ignorant about the use o' small arms."

"There's no need of finding Jem Larabee, Kirby," Stella said. "Ben will look after us. You can depend on it, we'll be well protected."

"Very well," Kirby said. "Snuff those lamps. All of 'em. No use wasting oil. I believe we're ready to pull out."

They knew that what he really meant was that he didn't care to have them outlined against the light when they left the house. However, their departure from Rolling Stone Manor was not challenged.

Kirby took the arms of Norah Logan and Stella and led the way. They all had expected that he would follow the back streets. Instead he headed for the lights of Lincoln Street.

"Ain't this bein' a little public?" Carhart objected. "Everybody in town will know Stella an' Timmy are in the Dakota House. Includin' whoever is after 'em."

"Exactly," Kirby said. "I want them to know." He added, "There's safety in numbers. Who's going to take a shot at any of us with all these people around?"

They mingled with pedestrians on the thronged sidewalks of the gambling line. Many of the strollers were Horace Logan's visitors, still wearing their banquet garb. The Easterners were in a holiday mood, for this was their last night in Antler. They were to be taken to end of steel in the morning and, after that, they would entrain for home.

They were determined to make the most of their time and were viewing the night life of a boom town at first hand. Groups of them, including women, were invading the music houses and saloons — a shocking breach of custom. Refined members of the gentler sex were usually rigidly excluded from these places. But the visi-

190

tors had taken over the town for the night and convention was being ignored. Women in silk and satin and their escorts in starched linen and immaculate evening dress were rubbing elbows with painted percentage girls in dance halls and sitting in gambling games alongside tinhorns and buffalo hunters and loud-mouthed paddies from the construction crews.

They passed the Four Aces, but Kirby hurried his charges to the Dakota House.

"We'll be all right now," Norah said when they reached the hotel.

But Kirby accompanied them upstairs to the Logan rooms. Taking the key from Norah, he unlocked the door and thrust it open with his foot. He was remembering the explosive trap that Pete Jennings had tried to set at the Buffalo Hotel. However, there was no sign of danger.

He and Carhart moved through the rooms, guns in their hands. The suite was silent. Neither Horace Logan nor Norah's brother was present. Housemaids had turned down the covers on the beds and left the lamps burning low.

"All right," Kirby said. "There's nothing to be afraid of. Don't let anyone in until you're absolutely positive of who they are."

"You don't actually believe they'd try to

— to — ?" Norah began, but couldn't put it in words. "Here at the hotel?"

"From what we've seen already, they'll try anything now," Kirby said. "And don't forget that you're tarred with the same brush as the rest of us, as far as they're concerned. You've been doing too much talking to me. They know that. And they figure you know too much by this time."

He suddenly said, "Got any guns here?"

"G-g-guns?"

"It's time that we started shooting back," Kirby said. "All of us."

"There's a pistol in Father's room, I'm sure," she said shakily. "And possibly one in Reid's."

"Find them."

She complied and presently returned with two pistols. Kirby made sure they were loaded and capped. "All right," he said. "If you have to shoot, aim for the belly. That stops them fast."

"Where are you going?" Stella asked protestingly.

"I'm curious about what Carhart said was going on at your place. I want to take a look. I'll be back."

"Go with him, Ben," Stella said. "He might need you. We'll be safe here." She smiled wanly.

Kirby heard Stella lock the door back of them as they left the room. "There's one thing I'm sure for real certain," Carhart said when they reached Lincoln Street, "an' that is that I'm in deeper water than I figured when I put my toes in."

"Want to wade out?"

"If it'll help Stella an' Timmy," Carhart said, "I'm stickin'. Stella's had somethin' bearin' down real hard on her lately. She's been scared. Too scared to talk about it."

"She's in as deep as I am," Kirby said. "But you owe me nothing."

"Bein' as I never laid eyes on you 'til to-night, friend, I can't say I do. But Stella seems to think mighty high o' you. An' so did Lee. An' that purty Logan gal acts like she trusts you. That's a lot o' votes in your favor."

Carhart added, "Lee Venters was a mighty good friend o' mine."

Chapter 11

They walked in silence toward the Four Aces, stepping aside occasionally to avoid boisterous groups of visitors. The Four Aces, with its lack of percentage girls and bawdy features, was not as attractive to the sight-seers as the more lurid establishments. Still, the tables were busy and many Easterners were trying their luck at the games.

Kirby paused on the sidewalk. "Is there a rear door? A side door. With a place for a lookout?"

"Sure," Carhart said. "Follow me."

They left Lincoln Street and moved down a passageway between the knock-down walls of the Four Aces and an ad-joining fandango house where music blared. Carhart unlocked a door in the darkness and it admitted them to a small room that served as the business office for the Four Aces.

The room was deserted, but a swinging lamp burned overhead. Carhart lowered the lamp and turned down the wick. He moved aside a small picture on the wall, exposing a peephole.

"Take a peek," he said. "There's another of these look-sees that I'll use."

Kirby placed an eye to the opening. He had a view down the length of the casino. Business was brisk. Faro, Spanish monte, poker, and the roulette game were in action.

Eight or ten drinkers stood at the bar. Kirby decided that the two bartenders were laboring under a strain, for they kept looking toward the door of the office as though hoping someone would appear and take over responsibility. They were expecting Stella, of course. Or Carhart.

Carhart was peering from another peephole. "There are two of 'em at the bar," he muttered. "Looks like nothin' happened yet. There's that bandy-legged one, an' the other in a leather vest. An' across the room at the birdcage game is another of 'em. Him with the peaked hat an' checkered shirt."

"I know that one, at least," Kirby said. "Bart Allen. The Vigilantes ran him out of San Francisco and I deadlined him a year or so ago at Lovelock. That's a railroad town in Nevada Territory. He was posing as a gambler, but was really earning his money by highway robberies and footpad work."

"From their looks that's the life story of all of 'em," Carhart said. "There are two more at that rear poker table, actin' drunk an' ugly. All of 'em are new in Antler."

Kirby became aware that action at the tables was a little hectic, with stakes higher than usual. This, probably, was due to the presence of the visitors. They were moneyed men who were pushing the play. But it added to the tension and helped divert attention from the noisy toughs.

However, uneasiness seemed to touch patrons here and there, for men were cashing in their chips and drifting out of the place.

The heavy drinking and loud talk continued, along with outbursts of profanity. The pair at the bar were quarreling and the two at the poker table were also passing ugly talk.

The two at the bar came to the point of physical battle, but were separated by the bartenders who ordered them to quiet down or leave the place. They subsided, but only for a short time.

"Fred an' Tim have got their woes tonight," Carhart muttered. "Them's the barkeeps. Good men, but they ain't gunfighters. They're wonderin' why in blazes I don't show up to back them up. They know there's real trouble on the way."

"This has been going on for quite a spell," Kirby commented. "It must be an hour since you came to the Venters' house. Those men aren't drunk, of course. They're only pretending. But they're getting thirsty and bored."

"I don't understand it," Carhart said.

"They've been stalling for time. They're waiting for someone and he hasn't shown up as soon as expected."

"Who?"

Kirby shrugged. "That's the question."

They waited. But not for long. Kirby sighed. "Maybe we'll soon know something."

Parson Slate had entered the Four Aces.

Kirby watched Slate move to the bar and order whisky and bitters with a mineral water chaser. Slate finished his drink without haste, then sauntered among the tables, pausing here and there to watch the play.

"Key man!" Carhart whispered excitedly. "He's passin' the wink to the wolf pack. They're all watchin' him."

"The executioner, maybe," Kirby said. "He's the one who'll give the sign to touch off the —"

He went quiet. Two newcomers had entered. One was Martin Garrett, the shaggy-browed vice-president of Grand Pacific. Garrett wore his evening dress, but his companion, who was a stranger to Kirby, had on a dark sack suit, black string tie and white cotton shirt. He was a man of about forty-five, sparsely fleshed, with prominent cheekbones and sandy hair.

And he sported a long, waxed, spike mustache.

Kirby exclaimed, "That one with Martin Garrett? Do you know him?"

"By reputation," Carhart said. "He was pointed out to me some time back as the expert on surveyin' an' locatin' railroads. That's Raymond Coleman. He located the route the Grand Pacific is buildin'. He's got a real big name in railroadin'."

Kirby took a long, deep breath. The pseudo Raymond Coleman had come out of hiding at last. He watched as Martin Garrett led his companion to a row of chairs that stood along the rear wall for the convenience of drinkers who did not want to remain at the bar.

Parson Slate was still drifting, apparently aimlessly, among the tables. Kirby never let his eyes leave the gunman. Slate strolled past the line of chairs. He drew a handkerchief from a pocket as though to mop his brow, but dropped the cloth.

Dropped it directly in front of where the fake Raymond Coleman sat. Slate stooped, picked up the handkerchief and spoke to the man in the chair, as though apologizing. Then Slate moved on.

It had all been deliberate. A signal. The marking of a man for death.

Ben Carhart had been watching, too. "My God!" he breathed. "It can't be Coleman that's to be —"

"Look!" Kirby exclaimed.

Reid Logan had entered the casino from the street. He was alone. He, too, was still in evening dress, but was bareheaded as though he had come hurrying on some unexpected call. He paused inside the door, gazing around as though seeking someone in the busy gambling room.

He apparently located his objective, for he started down the room, working his way among the bystanders at the tables, heading toward the rear of the room.

Kirby suddenly left his viewpoint and rushed to the door which opened into the gambling room. It was locked, but the key was in the lock and that delayed him a second or two before he wrenched it open.

Reid Logan was within a dozen feet of him, his back turned. He was moving toward the counterfeit Raymond Coleman, who sat alone in the line of chairs. Martin Garrett had gone to the bar to bring drinks to their chairs.

Many things happened simultaneously in the next moment. The quarrelsome pair at the poker table burst into wild action. One seized a chair and, with a howl of fury, swung a wild blow that missed his supposed opponent. However, its arc smashed a cluster of reflector oil lamps overhead.

At the bar, a gunfight exploded, with six-shooters roaring deafeningly. The pair at the poker table also went for their weapons and began shooting.

Players and spectators dived to the floor, plunging beneath tables or holding chairs as shields against stray bullets.

More lamps were shot out. Kirby caught Reid Logan in a sprawling dive that sent them both toppling to the floor into the uncertain shelter of the roulette table.

Kirby again had the sensation of living over a moment from Omaha. On that occasion it had been Horace Logan whose life he had tried to save by a similar action.

As he carried Reid Logan to cover he had the impression that the pseudo Raymond Coleman, who had leaped to his feet, was pitching forward to the floor, grasping his stomach, a horrified disbelief in his face.

Reid Logan twisted around and recognized Kirby. "What in the name of — ?" he began in a fury.

A bullet tore into the leg of the roulette table, showering him with splinters, silencing him.

"Roll man!" Kirby panted. "Crawl! Farther under the table. They're after you. They've already got that other one, from the looks."

He realized that he also was a target for a slug smashed into the plank floor within inches of his face. He elbowed himself desperately, jamming Reid Logan deeper into shelter beneath the table. Another bullet ricocheted between them.

Kirby's gun was in his hand. He twisted around, seeking a target. All he could see were the pallid faces and huddled forms of other men who were crouching beneath adjoining tables. Above them, guns continued to explode, but Kirby was unable to pick out the weapon that was being aimed at the roulette table.

The shooting ended, but not the uproar. Men were shouting and fighting to reach the doors. "Fire! Fire! Let's get out of here!"

The murky light through the fog of gunsmoke no longer came from the lamps. Flames were leaping up in several places from pools of oil where bullets had shattered the bowls.

"This way!" Kirby panted. "Keep your blasted head down! Do you still want to have your brains blown out, if you've got any?"

He pushed Reid Logan ahead of him, forcing him to scramble crab-fashion on his knees, toward the door to the office. Other men were crowding through it ahead of them. The flames were spreading fast.

Caught in the human tide, they were swept through the office and into the open at the rear of the building where they managed to fight their way clear of the stampede.

Reid Logan tried to pause and catch his breath, but Kirby would not allow that until he had dragged him almost bodily around the corner of a shed where they were in shadow.

"Are you crazy?" Reid gasped.

Flames were already bursting through the roof of the Four Aces. Apparently all the patrons had escaped, for the panicky shouting had ended. The office door of the casino was open and lighted by the glow of the fire inside.

Kirby started to race toward that pathway into the burning building, but he had taken only a few strides when he halted. He was too late. Long tongues of flame whipped through the opening and licked at the outer wooden walls. The fire was creating its own furnace-draught.

Reid overtook him. "What were you going to do? Not go back in there? Why?"

"To bring out a man," Kirby said. "If he was still alive, which I doubt."

"A man? Who was he?"

"The one your father knows as Raymond Coleman."

He led Reid deeper into the shadows of a shed. "Don't make a target of yourself," he warned. "He'll try again if he can notch on you."

"Who?"

"Parson Slate. I'm sure he was the one who was trying to kill us after he got the other one."

"Are you trying to say — ?"

"Why did you come to the Aces?" Kirby demanded.

"Because I wanted to talk to Raymond Coleman and find out if what you said about the railroad was true."

"But how did you know he would be at the Aces at this time? He's been a pretty slippery customer."

"A note from Martin Garrett was handed to me while I was showing a party of visitors the sights of the town. Garrett said he had located Coleman and they would wait for me to join them for a drink at the Four Aces."

"Garrett?" That suddenly cleared up many puzzles. Kirby looked at the Four Aces. It was a bonfire. Flames had spread to the neighboring honky-tonk whose canvas top exploded in a billow of fire. Locomotive whistles were screeching in the Grand Pacific yards, calling all hands to meet the emergency. The horns of volunteer fire crews were sounding. Antler was mobilizing to battle a foe that might destroy it.

"Ever hear of a cross-fire?" Kirby asked. "You were to be killed — by accident. A stray bullet."

"You *must* be making this up."

"And I was just making up those slugs somebody was sending your way. Somebody brought in a gang of paid ruffians lately and mobilized them in the Aces tonight with orders to start a fake gunfight when the signal was given, and to see that the place burned down. Under cover of the shooting, you and your fake Raymond

Coleman were to be knocked off."

"You saw this man I believed to be Raymond Coleman. He *wasn't* the real Raymond Coleman?"

"That's right. Even his mustache wasn't much like the one Ray used to wear."

"But why would they want to kill *him?* He was one of them."

"Only hired to take orders," Kirby said. "Small potatoes in their scheme of things." He gestured toward the burning casino. "He was a danger to them. They knew he'd be exposed, sooner or later. Probably sooner, now that they figured we were getting onto their crookedness. So they decided to get rid of him. Shooting out the lamps to burn the Aces was part of it. Nobody will ever be able to identify him now, or say he isn't the real Ray Coleman. And you came within a whisker of being in that fire with him."

"But, why would they want to kill me?"

"As an example."

"Example? Of what?"

"A warning, rather. Like the one Stella Venters had. Her husband was murdered. They tried to grab Timmy in order to hold a club over Stella's head to keep her from talking. Even if any of us do get to Horace Logan in time to tell him the truth, they

205

want the same kind of a club to keep him quiet."

"I can't believe any man would do things like that."

"Believe what you want. This is no poker game. And we're up against more than one man. A pack. They blooded their hands when they had Lee Venters killed. They won't hesitate to spill the blood of anyone who stands in their way. They're playing for millions. That's what the Grand Pacific will be worth."

"Do you mean they'd try to bulldoze my father by putting me out of the way? He'd never knuckle down. You should know him well enough to know that."

"He has a daughter," Kirby said. "Stella Venters has a daughter. Stella knuckled down."

"Good God! Do you mean they'd threaten to harm Norah?"

"Not only threaten, they'd go through with it. Can't I get it through your head that this game is for keeps?"

Reid peered at him, their faces lighted by the crimson reflection of the flames. Both the Four Aces and the honky-tonk were blazing furiously. Bucket lines were in action to prevent spread of the fire.

"Who are they?" Reid asked.

"Inchman, for one. And others. But there's no proof."

"Of course, of course!" Reid exclaimed. "So that's the way they're working it! Why, they're in a position to take over the Grand Pacific almost overnight."

"How's that?"

"Inchman poses as being alone, but Dad told me only today that he's really only the agent for a group of financial pirates. Dad learned just lately that Inchman's group has been working secretly for months to buy control of one company after another that holds our contracts. Two steel mills in Ohio, a logging outfit that supplies our ties, the commissary firm that furnishes our provisions. Even the steamboat line that operates between here and St. Louis that helps bring in food."

"I see," Kirby said.

"Of course, you see. As preferred creditors these companies would just about take over the Grand Pacific in a receivership at a few cents on the dollar. They'd soon own everything lock, stock, and barrel."

Reid said suddenly, "I'm not armed. Would you mind loaning me your pistol, McCabe?"

"I *would* mind. It'd be signing your death warrant."

"I'll do the worrying about that."

"You intend to hunt up Inchman and accuse him of things you can't really prove. You're going to give Parson Slate the excuse to make up for missing you when he tried to drill you tonight in the Aces."

"Loan me your gun, please."

"Inchman's no fool. He'll figure that you'll be coming after him. He knows the Logans. They're knights in armor. With white plumes. Pure gold, and brave. They ask no odds, no favors. They fight their battles singlehanded."

He glared at Reid. "Have you forgotten how your father came into the Four Aces that night in Omaha in his shining armor and plumes to have it out with Inchman? And how Parson Slate was planted across the room to shoot him in the back?"

"I'm afraid our plumes are a sorry sight," Reid admitted dryly. "Thanks for the warning. I'm doubly armored. Now, the pistol."

Kirby had to laugh — helplessly. "You *are* a knucklehead! I'm keeping the gun. And that's that. Let's go."

"Go where?"

"To find Inchman — if he's to be found."

"But you just said — !"

"I know what I just said. If we find Inchman, we'll likely also find Parson Slate. If you pack a gun, it'll be a case of self-defense or of protecting Inchman's life, if Slate back-shoots you. Just as it was in Omaha with your father. If you're unarmed, they won't dare kill you openly. That would be murder. I'll pack the gun."

"Oh, no you don't. Who's wearing the white plumes now? What's to stop them from shooting *you* in the back. This isn't your affair. It's our fight."

"Wrong. I'm in this. Lee Venters was my friend. And there's Stella. And Timmy. It also happens that I don't want Horace Logan killed. At least, not yet."

"Shiloh? McCabe, do you still — ?"

"Yes, Shiloh. I want the truth of it. From him."

"You really believe they might kill him?"

"It's possible, though I imagine they'd prefer to wait until he's charmed his trainload of dudes out of their money. Inchman's crowd would rather lose other people's cash than their own, I'm sure. When they take over, they'll abandon that stretch beyond Shiloh River, write off the loss, and build north of Squaw Buttes. And probably die very, very rich."

Kirby paused. "They'll try to silence

anyone who might upset their wagon — Horace Logan included. I would advise you to look him up and warn him. That yarn about him being under the weather is another of the pack of lies I've been getting from your side of the fence."

"Garrett did that to protect him," Reid Logan said. "He told Norah and me later on that Father was all right. But, as far as warning him goes, I doubt if it's necessary, tonight at least. He should be safe enough at Shiloh River."

"Shiloh River? Isn't he here in Antler?"

"He left for the steel camp a while ago on a special run. He wanted to make sure everything was ready for visitors. And he did need a rest and to get away from them for one night."

Kirby realized that Horace Logan probably had been on his way to board the train for Shiloh River when he had ridden past in the carriage earlier. "Are you sure he got on that train?" he demanded.

"Positive. I saw him aboard. They'd loaded the tent on a flatcar, and Dad wanted to make sure it was pitched properly and ready for the party."

"If I were you," Kirby said, "I'd see to it that your sister also got out of Antler. At once. Tonight. Hide her somewhere until this thing is settled one way or another. If possible, take Stella and Timmy with her."

"And if you were me, you wouldn't try," Reid said. "I don't want to lose the only arm I've got. Or have my eyes scratched out. Norah has a mind of her own."

"That's no answer. With her out of their reach, they'd have no way of twisting your father to their purpose."

"You don't know her. She'd soar like a rocket if I tried anything like that."

"Another damned Logan in shining armor," Kirby snorted. "You ought to clear out also."

"If you think I'm going to run from these thugs, you're very mistaken," Reid snapped.

Angry and excited, he was moving at a long stride, forcing Kirby to keep pace with him. Lincoln Street was a whirlpool of activity, of hectic bucket lines, of shouting and the thumping of the pump bars on the fire equipment that had been dragged to the scene. The Four Aces and the honky-tonk were being left to burn to the ground, but water was flooding adjoining structures.

"Just where are we bound?" Kirby asked.

"To find Inchman, of course. That's what you just said."

"And where would that be?"

"At the Dakota House, probably."

"I've got a better idea. Where would we be most likely to find your Grand Pacific vice-president, Martin Garrett?"

Reid came to a sudden stop. "Wait a blasted minute, McCabe! You're not saying . . . ?"

The words faded off. He stood looking at Kirby in despair. "Tell me," he breathed, "is there anything a person can believe in? Anybody a man can trust? Not Martin Garrett! Why, my father thinks the world of him, trusts him completely."

"Garrett brought the fake Raymond Coleman to the Aces tonight," Kirby said. "He saw to it that the man was seated in a position to be murdered in the cross-fire. He made sure he was in the clear before the shooting started. He also wrote the note that brought you there to be killed, my friend."

Chapter 12

Kirby watched disillusionment and bitterness grow in Reid Logan's expression. "It's my guess Inchman and Garrett will be getting together this minute, figuring out their next play. They've got problems that are growing harder to figure out. They got their fake Ray Coleman out of the way, but they've missed on rubbing me out, and on taking care of you. The only thing they can be sure of is that your father still doesn't know that Garrett has run the Grand Pacific down a blind switch."

"The telegraph wire," Reid said. "I'll go to the depot, and —"

"And get your head shot off," Kirby said. "They'll be smart enough to think of that and will have some of their slingers on watch there. Don't you understand that we have got to keep our heads off the skyline?"

"You say it like you're discussing the weather," Reid said angrily.

"Not exactly. But we've got to find these two gentlemen together, and do it before they find us. Together, you understand, in order to make sure they're in cahoots. There's always the chance that we might be wrong about Garrett. Circumstantial evidence is mighty tricky."

"They both are staying at the Dakota House," Reid argued. "They'll be either in Inchman's quarters or Garrett's."

"That's too obvious. In addition, they're watching the Dakota House, knowing Stella and Timmy are there in the Logan rooms. We'd be picked off."

"There's a big root cellar with an outside entrance into a supply shed fifty feet or more from the hotel," Reid said. "We used it in getting the food ready for the banquet in the tent. I'm sure we could get in through the cellar without being seen."

"I say the Dakota House is still too obvious a meeting place. We're dealing with shrewd people. They'll figure that we might be looking for them. They'll steer clear of the Dakota House — especially if they've got shooters there to knock us off. They want to be as far away as possible, personally, from any killings that take place."

"You're probably right. If so, we won't have much chance of finding them."

"Find the woman," Kirby said.

"Woman?"

"A man like Inchman usually is involved with a woman. I know nothing about Garrett, but I'll gamble that he has a soft shoulder to lean on also at times."

Reid snapped his fingers. "You're right. A dark-eyed wench. The kind that live by their wits. But attractive. Very. Not a percentage girl, or a dance hall harpie. More style than that. Much more. Slender, very black hair. Might be a touch of Spanish in her."

"This is Garrett's woman? How do you know?"

"Saw them dining last night in a place called the Silver Moon. I only got a glimpse of them in a curtained booth. I was with a party of Easterners who were seeing the sights and we left the place right afterward."

"Name?"

"I didn't try to find out. It wasn't any of my business at the time. I didn't want to know anything. Garrett has a wife back East. I've met her."

Jem Larabee was directing fire-fighting operations nearby. Kirby touched the railroad detective on the shoulder. "Who's the prettiest of the gay gals in town?" he asked. "One with black hair and eyes, who wouldn't give you the time of day unless you had a fat bank account and knew how to pick out nice presents for a girl — such as a purse with a chunk of money in it now and then."

Larabee mopped sweat from his face, punched back his hat and frowned. "There'd be two, three ladies that might answer to that brand," he said. "Dark-eyed, dark-haired, you say."

Reid nodded. "Very. She'd have to be the kind of a woman who might catch the eye of an important man — such as Martin Garrett."

Larabee's frown deepened. He debated whether to answer. "That," he finally said slowly, "would be Dolly Prince. She's had other names in other places."

"Where does she hang out?"

"Now, Dolly's never caused no trouble, and —"

"Where can we find her? This is important."

"Frame cottage on Second Street," Larabee said. "Second Street crosses Lincoln at the corner where the Silver Moon stands. Turn south about half a block. Cottage stands back from the street. Clapboard-built with a little porch. There's —"

He no longer had listeners. Kirby and Reid were on their way. But Ben Carhart's voice called, "Wait!"

Carhart came hurrying to overtake them. "I'm mighty happy to see you still alive an' kickin'," he said to Kirby. "You too, Mr. Logan. I lost track o' you when the shootin' started. Been lookin' for you. What — ?"

"We've got no time for a powwow now, Ben," Kirby said. "Later. Hustle back to the hotel and stick with the Venters and Miss Logan. Make sure they stay in that room. Don't let them wander out. The batter's thickened even more since we last saw you."

They left Carhart and hurried onward. Reid halted suddenly, and said, "Just a minute!"

He retraced his steps, overtaking Carhart, while Kirby waited. The two spoke briefly in the darkness, then Reid returned at a run and rejoined Kirby.

They located the cottage on the unlighted side street. It had more character than its scattered neighbors. At least it was freshly painted, and its approach was neat. There were flower boxes on the little porch.

Lights burned inside, but heavy curtains were drawn. They tiptoed nearer. Some of the windows were open for the sake of coolness. They heard the faint resonance of men's voices.

Before Kirby could stop him, Reid mounted the porch and knocked on the door. The voices halted abruptly. Kirby, crouching below an open window, heard whispers. Reid knocked again.

Evidently a decision was made to respond. Kirby heard the rustle of a dress. The door was opened.

"Yes?" a woman's voice demanded. She uttered a little gasp and tried to slam the door.

Reid blocked that. "Sorry, lady! I'm coming in!"

Kirby mounted silently to the porch and stepped in at Reid's heels. The door admitted them to a small entry hall. A curtained archway to the left led to the parlor. There was a smaller door opening at the rear of the hall, also closed by drapes, which evidently opened into a dining room or kitchen.

Dolly Prince stood aside, angry, but not exactly frightened. Apparently she had seen enough of violence in her life to be hardened to it.

Reid parted the drapes and stood looking into the parlor. "Well, if it isn't Mr. Garrett!" he said. "The kind of company you keep."

Kirby murmured to Dolly Prince. "Stay out of this! Stay where you are!"

He remained out of sight of the parlor, letting Reid carry the play.

"What do you mean, forcing your way into this house, Logan?" Martin Garrett demanded. There was the thickness of panic in his voice.

"Hello, Inchman," Reid said.

The oily voice of Barney Inchman responded. "Good evening. Is there anything we can do for you?"

"Not any longer," Reid said. "All I wanted was to make sure you two reptiles were in this together."

Inchman lifted his voice a trifle. "Dolly! Close that outside door!"

Kirby shook his head in an order not to obey. Inchman's voice sharpened. "Is someone else there with you?"

The woman took a chance and answered, "Yes."

As she spoke, she crouched, huddling closer against a wall. She was staring, frightened, at the curtained rear door. Kirby saw the curtains part slightly.

His gun was in his hand, but Reid was in his line of fire. "Duck!" he snapped. "Deadfall! To your right!"

Reid whirled. His reaction was deadly

swift. A six-shooter was in his hand, although Kirby had believed that he was unarmed.

Reid fired an instant before a gun exploded in the slit between the curtains. Kirby was dodging. Nevertheless, he felt the sharp twinge of a wound on his upper left arm. The slug had missed Reid, but he had been nicked.

Reid kept pouring bullets into the curtain as fast as he could rock the hammer with his thumb.

Another shot had bellowed from the opening in the curtains, but the powderflame had gushed toward the ceiling. Plaster fell.

Reid stopped shooting. Both he and Kirby plunged ahead and tore the drapes aside. A man lay there, quivering in his last moments of life. Then he lay still.

He was small and sharp-featured, with a pointed nose. Kirby remembered Jem Larabee's description of a gunman who had been helping Parson Slate guard Inchman. This must have been the one known as The Sparrow.

The gunman evidently had been struck just over the heart by the first bullet Reid had fired into the curtain. At least one other slug had pierced him, but the man had been dying when he had fallen.

Dolly Prince screamed, but remained huddled in fear against the wall. Barney Inchman sat frozen in an armchair in the parlor. He was armed, but had made no move toward his holster. Martin Garrett had risen partly to his feet. Now he sank back onto a sofa. He was ashen.

Reid moved into the parlor. "Draw!" he said. "I've got two slugs left in this. Draw! Either of you. Or both. I'd like to get both of you off the back of my father and off of Grand Pacific's back."

Neither man moved. Kirby stood ready to join in, if a fight came. He doubted if there were two live shells left in Reid's pistol. One perhaps. Or possibly none.

But Barney Inchman, who probably knew this, preferred not to take a chance. He merely sat motionless, keeping his hands hard-gripped on the arms of his chair.

Reid spoke to Garrett. "You leech! You bite the hand that feeds you. My father trusted you. You Judas!"

He spoke to Kirby without looking away from the two in the parlor. "Any idea who was the one out there?"

"One of Inchman's bodyguards, I think," Kirby said. "A slinger called The Sparrow, I believe."

"Well, our business here is finished," Reid said.

They backed out of the hallway. Dolly Prince had straightened, deciding that she was safe from gunfire.

"Send for the marshal to take care of the body," Kirby told her. "Tell him anything, as long as you tell him the truth. And only the truth. Remember that we'll be back to check up on you."

He and Reid left the cottage. A few heads showed at windows and dark doorways along the street, but no citizens ventured into the opening. Evidently events at Dolly Prince's house were matters to be treated with extreme caution.

"Where did you get that shootin iron?" Kirby demanded.

"Borrowed it from Ben Carhart. That's what I went back to him for. The debt grows bigger."

"What debt?"

"You seem to make a career of saving the lives of Logans, McCabe. You warned me just in time there in that house. Can't I make you understand that we'd prefer to be left to fight our own battles?"

"I'd be happy to do just that thing from now on. This last one was cutting it mighty thin. Inchman's shooters can't always miss.

Fact is, they didn't entirely miss this time. I don't mind losing some blood, but it's going to ruin my shirt, and shirts cost money."

The left sleeve of Kirby's shirt was stained crimson. The twitch of the bullet on his upper arm had been more than a graze. The slug had plowed a gouge through flesh. It was a relatively minor injury, but it was bleeding freely.

"Why didn't you tell me you were hit, you fool?" Reid exclaimed.

"I'm telling you now. All it needs is a bandage and someone who knows how to tie it on. Could you — ?"

He broke off, discomfited, realizing that his companion had only one arm.

"Don't try to spare my feelings," Reid raged. "I know I'm a cripple."

"Only in your head when you talk like that."

"All right, all right! We'll find a doctor."

"Doctor, my eye. It's only a scratch. I've been hurt worse by snow mosquitoes in the Sierra Nevadas. And lost more blood, to boot. Besides, the lid is off now. Inchman will turn the wolf loose for certain. They've got to blast us, or see the whole kettle of fish spilled. If we go around trying to find a doctor, we'll find something that'll make it so we won't ever need a doctor at all."

Reid, despite Kirby's protests, struck a match and took a look at the injury. "You bleed real nice," he commented. "Won't get any blood poison, at least. It's a pretty good furrow, an' it's got to be taken care of. One one-armed man is all I want to deal with in this life."

"We've got to lay mighty low," Kirby said. He was moving ahead toward the railroad yards.

"You seem to have an idea?"

"How about that palace car of your dad's where I had a palaver with Garrett? Is that still dark?"

"I should have thought of it myself," Reid said. "The very place."

They made their way through dark areas to the railroad yards, crossed several lines of tracks and finally located the palace car. It still stood alone on the dead spur on the bluff above the rushing Missouri River. It was dark and silent.

"Couldn't be a lonelier place," Kirby commented.

Reid had a key which admitted them to the car. "Better not light a lamp," he said. "I'll find some towels to hold over that arm. I won't be gone long. Sit until

I get back. In the dark."

"Where are you going? Be careful nobody sees — !"

But Reid was already gone. Kirby padded his arm in the towels Reid had found. There was nothing to do but wait and fume.

The fire in Lincoln Street had died down so that only a haze of smoke marked the location. Business evidently was resuming, for he could hear the faint sound of music at times.

He was restless, but helpless. The irony of it again struck home. He was now taking shelter, in fear of his life, in the private car of the man he had come to Antler to destroy. Around him again was the opulent smell of success and money and luxury — the sort of existence that Horace Logan considered his birthright.

Footsteps were approaching the car. Reid's voice called cautiously, "McCabe?"

"Here, and bleeding to death," Kirby answered. "Where in hell have you been?"

Several persons entered the car in the darkness. "I brought Norah to wrap up that scratch," Reid explained. "And I thought it best to bring Mrs. Venters and her daughter, too. And Ben Carhart. There's safety in numbers. In addition, this car is going to be hooked to the excursion train and taken to Shiloh River tomorrow. I decided it was just as well that we got aboard under cover of darkness."

"You may be right," Kirby said. "But are you sure nobody saw you? Five people make quite a parade."

"I think we made it," Reid said confidently. "I went in by way of the underground supply tunnel. We came out that way. I'm sure we got away with it."

"Light a lamp, Reid. I can't see him in the dark," Norah said.

"That won't do," her brother said. "Somebody will spot a light in this car and come prying."

"Draw the curtains, idiot."

"Light might still show. How about the pantry? There's only one small window. We can cover that with blankets."

Kirby felt Norah's fingers touch his shoulder. She guided him down the length of the car and through a narrow door into the small pantry. It had not been used in days and the stove was cold.

There was only a porthole window. Kirby stood aside in the cramped quarters while she covered it with a blanket. She lighted a lamp.

"May I help?" Stella asked.

"There isn't room," Norah said. "Anyway, it doesn't look like he's going to cash in his chips very soon."

She had changed to a dark, serviceable dress and had her hair held in a snood. She had brought bandages and scissors, along with medical lotions. She bent close, using a purge to cleanse the bullet crease.

Kirby recoiled from the sharp sting of the liquid. "God Almighty! What is that? Greek fire?"

"Don't be such a baby!" she scoffed. "It's only liniment." She cut away the sleeve of his shirt so as to be able to operate more freely. "Keep your voice down. If you have to groan, do it under your breath."

She hesitated, then added, "I'm afraid we were followed from the hotel. I had a feeling someone was trailing us. And Ben Carhart has some other bad news for you. He'll tell you about it."

She bent closer while she adjusted the bandage. "Will you please stop squirming. It surely can't hurt that much. And I'm about finished."

Her hair brushed his cheek. He felt suddenly alive.

"What is it?" she asked, looking up.

"Nothing!" Kirby said. But there was a

sudden wildness in him. He had found himself wanting to take her in his arms, say soft things to her. But she was still Horace Logan's daughter.

"Make it fast!" he commanded harshly. "It's only a scratch, like you said, not a case of life-and-death."

She must have known what was raging within him. He suspected that she deliberately lingered over her task.

"All right," she finally said. "You're glued back together again. Reid brought one of his shirts for you. The one you're wearing is a sight. I believe his should fit fairly well. At least, it'd be an improvement."

With her scissors, she cut away his own, hard-used shirt, then helped him don a fresh, white garment. She blew out the lamp and left the pantry. Kirby followed her into the length of the unlighted main car.

The revelry in town was increasing. Yelling and occasional warwhoops arose. Six-shooters were being touched off in the air now and then.

Reid Logan and Ben Carhart sat in leather armchairs, from which they kept watch, centering their attention mainly on the railroad yards and the buildings of the town.

The rooftops were outlined against the glow from Lincoln Street. They rose above the blocky shapes of a string of empty box-cars on a siding a few rods away. Farther down the yards, Kirby could make out the flutter of bunting on the dark chain of coaches that would carry the excursionists to Shiloh River in the morning.

His eyes tuned themselves to the dark-ness in the parlor car. He saw that Reid had a six-shooter in his lap and another lying on the floor within reach. Ben Carhart had a pistol. He also had a shotgun and a rifle leaning against the wall of the car. Stella and Timmy were sitting in the background. Norah joined them.

"Where did you round up all the artil-lery?" Kirby asked.

"At our rooms at the hotel," Reid said. "My father likes hunting and target shooting. He always carries his guns with him."

Kirby glanced at Norah, understanding how she had so readily produced pistols earlier at the hotel. "Expecting callers?" he asked Reid.

"Could be. Money talks, they say."

"Money?"

"Ever carry a price on your head, my friend?"

"Not that I recall," Kirby said slowly.

"You carry one now. A thousand in gold to anybody who dusts you for keeps. I assume there's a time limit on the bounty offer. You'd be no good dead if you happened to live long enough to spoil things for the payees."

"A thousand dollars? The misers. It ought to be worth ten times that to them. How do you know about this?"

"A friend of Ben, and of Mrs. Venters. Name of Fred Brackett. He's a dealer at the Four Aces. He also happens to know, personally, one of that crowd of gunmen that Inchman mustered at the Aces tonight. The gunman didn't like that business. It seems that Stella and Lee Venters had done him a favor back along the way somewhere. He tipped off Brackett that a price had been set on her head. And on yours. He even knew that Stella was at the Logan suite in the Dakota House and was being watched. Brackett came there and managed to sneak word to Stella. That was just before I showed up to bring them here."

"A price on *her* head? On Stella? They want her shot down too, along with us? A woman?"

He realized the implication of this. "Not

Timmy, too?" he asked.

"Yes, Timmy, too. Maybe not in so many words. After all, openly putting a price on the murder of a woman might be a little strong for even the stomachs of some of the toughs they've hired."

"But not for a man like Parson Slate," Kirby commented.

"And likely other of those hard cases. However, we're all in the same boat, Norah included. I hate to deflate you, McCabe, but your hair isn't worth a cent more than the top-knots of the rest of us."

"You've been here only a few days, and already you're slinging the lingo like a buffalo hunter," Kirby said.

"Never mind my lingo. Even Ben will be included in the bag, now," Reid said. "He knows too much by this time, just by association with the likes of us."

"That makes six scalps," Kirby said. "*Six!* Even little Timmy's! That's hard to believe!"

"Will you *please* stop referring to me as little Timmy!" Timmy said, annoyed. "I'm grown up."

"Too much for your own good," Reid said. "And too pretty too."

"Do you really think so? Now, that's the first time you've said anything nice to me," the girl murmured half in jest.

"Please let's not go into that now," Kirby said.

He looked around. "Six nice scalps worth a thousand apiece," he said musingly. "But they've got to get all of us. Any one of us can sink their ship for them. It's the whole bag or nothing for them. They know that."

He eased his wounded left arm on the chair. The injury was throbbing. "Six birds in a cage," he observed.

"Know of a better cage?" Reid asked.

"If they're looking for us, they might decide to take a look at Horace Logan's parlor car."

"Why should they be looking for us? They think the women, at least, are still at the hotel. They'll figure we'll show up there sooner or later and be laying for us there."

"It sounds good," Kirby said. He was remembering that Norah suspected they had been seen coming to the car.

"At any rate I don't picture them as wanting to touch off an open gunfight," Reid said. "Not here. And not tonight."

"What *do* you picture?"

"All they want is to keep us away from my father until this excursion train pulls out for Shiloh River. They'll try to see to it that we don't get on that train, or that we don't send any messages to him."

He added wryly, "It's just as you said. They'll want him to sell stock to his visitors. That will sweeten the kitty. It won't matter too much what happens after that."

Kirby spoke after a time. "How many men do you figure we might be up against? Ben, did your friend have anything to say along that line?"

"Nope," Carhart replied. "But if the word has been passed around in certain circles that there's easy money to be made in Antler, if a man don't mind poppin' a few caps an' burnin' a little gunpowder, your guess is as good as mine."

"Tell me," Norah said. "I'm very slow at guessing."

"I'll give it to you straight," Kirby said. "This isn't Lockport, Ohio. Nor is it Washington or New York. This is Dakota Territory."

"I believe I'm way ahead of you," Norah said.

"Sure. There're plenty of men in the West who don't care to soil their hands with honest work. Like Ben said, a thousand dollars is easy money to them and they don't care how they earn it. We already know we're up against five of that kind. We saw them in the Four Aces. There are probably more."

"Not counting Parson Slate," Reid commented.

"Your sister isn't as sure as you are that you people weren't trailed here from the hotel," Kirby said.

"What makes you say that, Norah?" Reid asked, startled.

"I can't say exactly," she admitted. "Imagination, maybe."

"There's a way of finding out," Kirby said.

He moved toward the door leading to the observation platform. Norah tried to stop him. "Don't be foolish!" she protested.

But he opened the door and stepped onto the platform. The festive spirit still prevailed in Lincoln Street, with six-shooters exploding at intervals.

Kirby did not permit himself to become an easy target. He kept moving around the rim of the platform, depending on the faint light to help protect him. He suddenly turned to retreat inside the door. It was a maneuver designed to hurry any nervous marksman who might be trying to notch a sight on him.

He succeeded. A rifle exploded. The bullet glanced wickedly from the metal frame of the door within inches of his face, stinging him with fragments. But he was unhurt as he dived inside the car, sprawling on the thick carpet.

"Stay down!" he snapped. "Keep your heads down!" Silence came. He could hear the suppressed breathing of the others. He finally crawled to the door, opened it, holding it jammed with his foot, and waved his hat, inviting a shot. None came.

He believed the rifle had been fired from between cars in the dark line of empty freighters that stood on the siding between the palace car and the town.

"There could be a dozen shooters hunkered along that string of boxes," Ben Carhart muttered, peering from a window. "If'n they start usin' rifles, they'll make a fishnet o' this car."

"No they won't," Reid said. "There's an inch of good strong sheet-iron between us."

"What do you mean?" Kirby asked.

"This car was originally built for Abraham Lincoln. Even the window glass distorts vision slightly. If we keep our heads down, they'll only waste lead trying to kill us by sheer fire power."

"They may try to force their way in," Stella spoke. Her voice was steady.

Kirby answered that. "That's when we'll have something to say about things. If they try it, you three ladies get into the pantry and stay there. We'll be shooting and we don't want to hit the wrong people. They'll never make it inside the car. After all, they're only fighting for money. That kind quit mighty easy."

But the silence went on. Nothing happened. Minutes passed. More minutes.

Norah was at Kirby's side, so close their shoulders brushed at times.

In the darkness he heard the murmur of Timmy's young, warm voice and Reid Logan answer in tones soft as velvet.

Kirby finally again moved to the door, opened it and waved his hat. There was no response. The wait continued.

He debated the thought of leaving the car and scouting the area. Ben Carhart argued against it. "It might be the old Injun trick of outlastin' the gopher," he said. "We're holed up here, safe an' snug. Why stick our nose out to be shot off? This car's supposed to be hauled to the steel camp. That's where we all want to go, ain't it? I say to sit tight."

The hours of high tension began to take

its toll. Kirby heard the soft breathing of Norah. She had fallen asleep, sitting on the carpet with her head cradled on her arms in the seat of a leather chair. Stella was dozing also, but Timmy was awake and staying close to Reid. He could hear their occasional whispering. Timmy even laughed softly at times.

Kirby remained awake. He was remembering the night before the battle opened at Shiloh. He had been sleepless all that night too, unable to ease the thought of what must come.

His nerves were on edge now. He did not believe this was over. More and more, he believed Ben Carhart had been right. They were still there in the darkness. Waiting and watching.

Finally, he could stand it no longer. Ignoring Carhart's objections, he crept to the door, across the platform and lowered himself to the ground.

The wind was drawing from the north. The Grand Pacific's machine shops, which were housed in low frame buildings, gave forth a steady, metallic cacophony a distance down the railroad yards. The thudding of trip-hammers came as a heavy heartbeat to the screeching of lathes and the whir of belts. The clang of steel rang from the boiler shop.

But no bullets came. He finally explored even the line of empty boxcars. No foe lurked there now. But they had been there and recently. The tang of chewing tobacco was strong in the air. But they were gone now.

He returned to the palace car. "They've pulled out," he said. "But they were there until a few minutes ago. Why did they leave?"

There was no answer. But he knew that his companions were relaxing, believing that it was over and that they had won. Soon, they were dozing again, and at times falling into deep sleep.

But he found himself vividly awake. He was cold, with a growing tension needling him. Why had they held vigil over the parlor car for so long, then faded away?

His senses, sharpened by the puzzle of the unanswered question, became tuned to every sound — apprehensively, suspiciously. There were many undertones that worked in and out of the medley from the railroad shops, rising above it at times, then dissolving into it.

Occasionally he made out the refrain of banjos and drums in the dance halls on Lincoln Street. He heard the coughing exhausts of yard engines, and the crash of couplings on the sidetracks where cars were being sorted and shunted. Boxcars and gondolas. Flats loaded with steel for Mike Callahan's crews at Shiloh River. Gondolas piled high with crossties that had been milled from timber floated down from the Black Hills. Power cars, their contents destined for the grading crews who were working west of the river into the country that would be a financial morass for Horace Logan.

He heard the dismal rush of the Missouri River below the bluff during lulls in the chorus.

In his ears, one sound began to dominate all others. It was the staccato coughing of a locomotive, whose throttle seemed to have been opened wide. The sound came from down the yards. He could hear the screech of tortured driving wheels that were spinning, not yet having gained traction. This eased and he knew the locomotive was picking up speed.

He came suddenly to his feet. He lifted Norah with him, shaking her awake.

"We've got to get out of here!" he exclaimed. "Everybody! Wake up! Wake up! We're in a trap! I'm sure of it!"

They seemed sluggishly inept as they

aroused. They framed questions in sleep-thick voices, questions for which he had no answer. All he knew was that they were in great danger. The roar of the oncoming engine was in his ears.

"Hurry! Hurry!" He dragged Stella to her feet and hurried her and Norah toward the door. "Get into the open! Get away from this car!"

"What — ?" Reid began. Then, as though realizing that Kirby must be implicitly obeyed, he lifted Timmy in his one arm, for she was having difficulty coming entirely awake.

Kirby's desperation galvanized them. They spilled to the ground and fled from the car. Kirby led the way at a run along the brushy margin of the river bluff.

The roar of the exhaust increased. Kirby saw the dark shape of the oncoming locomotive loom out of the background of switch lamps and lights from the town.

A heating furnace was tapped in the railroad shops, casting a crimson light against the sky. Kirby saw that the speeding locomotive was racing down the spur on which the palace car stood alone.

Collision was inevitable! "Down!" Kirby screeched. "That boiler may go like a bomb!"

He slid over the lip of the bank into brush, bringing Norah and Stella with him. "Flatten out!" he said. "Dig in!"

The others scrambled to shelter alongside. The wild-running locomotive thundered past above them and hurtled over the fifty-yard distance they had managed since leaving the car.

The crash had the heavy impact of a shot from a mighty cannon. There was the scream of torn metal.

That was submerged by the thunderclap of the boiler exploding. Kirby felt the ground lift a little. He threw himself across the bodies of Stella and Norah, clamping his arms around them to protect them as best he could.

The blast had deadened his eardrums temporarily. Even so, he could hear the faint screech of wreckage that was being hurled through the air. A rain of fragments crashed around them. But the heavier debris evidently had been thrown far beyond them in all directions. He heard splashes in the river as sizable fragments landed.

Along with that was the rending of brush and trees as the wreckage of the coach and what remained of the locomotive, locked together, went hurtling down the bluff into the river. A mighty splash came.

Then silence. All that Kirby knew was that he was still alive and apparently unhurt. Stella and Norah had also escaped. Reid had protected Timmy with his body. He had taken a bruise or two, but both he and Timmy rose to their knees, facing each other. Suddenly Reid kissed Timmy. They continued to stare at each other in unbelieving wonder. Ben Carhart had escaped with a lump on the head. He scoffed at it as unimportant, but Stella insisted on treating the injury.

"We've got to hide," Kirby said. "Hide deep. They may have seen us running from the car."

"Where can we go?" Norah asked.

"We don't dare go very far. The brush along the river might be our best bet. They might be hanging around. I understand now why they pulled out, after letting us know they were there. They didn't want to take a chance on being hit by this stuff that they knew would be flying around. They knew what was coming and had been sent there to keep us pinned down in that car."

"If they'd killed us, it would have been put down to another of these accidents they've been causing," Norah said.

"Thank you kindly, Stella," Carhart said when she ended her ministrations. "Say, I

242

sure got a right nice lump on my haid, didn't I? 'Minds me o' the day at Pittsburg Landin' when a chunk from one o' them big mortars on a Yank gunboat whapped me."

He added, with pride, "I was a gunner with the Fo'th Tennessee Volunteer Field Artillery."

The explosion seemed to have halted all sound and motion in Antler. The mechanical roar from the railroad shops had ceased. Now, as though a taut wire had snapped, shouting began in the town.

"Time to move," Kirby said. He led the way farther along the brink of the bluff, away from the scene of the explosion.

"Wouldn't it be better if we went back to the hotel?" Norah asked.

"That's what they'll expect, if there are any of us left alive," he said. "And I'm beginning to believe they think we all went into the river with what was left of that parlor car. Otherwise, I think they might have come after us. But they'll try to make sure. And we're not exactly in shape to stand much more of this. We need to hide out and decide what to do next. All this is coming too fast for me."

They could hear people running from town, shouting. A locomotive whistle

243

began wailing the distress signal down the yards.

They passed the bunting-draped excursion train on its spur. Except for a few broken windows it seemed to have escaped damage from the boiler blast. Kirby led the way a short distance farther and found a brushy hiding place on the river bank which offered a more comfortable refuge than their first covert.

They sank down in the thickets, utterly spent. Kirby could see the shine of the river through the trees down the slant below them. Mosquitoes began to torture them. Stella burst into tears.

Carhart patted her on the shoulder. "Don't you go a-breakin' down now, Stella," he said. "I got a feelin' we're about out o' the woods."

In the distance citizens were now swarming to the scene of the explosion. The refugees sat in silence, listening to the distant sounds. Reid pulled off his coat and wrapped it around Timmy.

"Let's hope they haven't called off the shindig at the steel camp on account of the wreck," Kirby said to the Logans. "Your father will learn of it by telegraph, of course, but he won't know his son and daughter were supposed to have been in the car when it went into the river."

"What difference would it make, even if it was called off?" Norah asked tiredly.

"This thing is about to come out in the open," Kirby said. "If we can make it to the steel camp, we'll have a better chance for our marbles. The boogy men aren't likely to be there. At least they won't outnumber us. Even if they show up, we'll have some fighting men on our side for a change. Mike Callahan, for instance. And some of those tough micks on the steel crews."

They all knew what he meant. If they reached Shiloh River alive.

"Once we can talk to my father, that will finish it," Norah said confidently.

Kirby hoped that she was right. But he doubted it. Barney Inchman would have his back to the wall, and from what Kirby had seen of the man, he did not believe there would be a meek surrender. Furthermore, Inchman might still have the backing of his paid gun hands.

But, even though that issue was settled there was still the one between himself and Horace Logan. Shiloh.

"We'll stay bushed up here for a while," he said. "You saw the coaches the dudes are going to ride that are spotted on a siding down the yards. Maybe we can stow away and get a free ride to Shiloh River without bumping into any of Inchman's shooters. At any rate, it'll be a lot better than sleeping in the brush all night."

"Maybe I have a better idea," Norah said. "A supply train will be going out several hours ahead of the excursion train. It will carry a coach for people who are going to help cook and wait table. I've hired a dozen or more ladies in town, and as many men, who will be aboard. I was supposed to go with them on that run. It might be better if we all went along. There'll be baggage cars loaded with supplies."

"But where — ?" Kirby began.

"I'm sure I saw it made up and standing on the same spur with the excursion train," Norah said. "Two baggage cars and a coach."

They huddled in their covert, listening to sounds in the distance. Railroad crews were assembling. Salvage equipment was being moved in. Torch baskets flamed. A heavy wrecking crane creaked past, pushed by a yard engine.

Reid spoke to Ben Carhart. "You mentioned fighting at Pittsburg Landing against the Yankees. I believe you said you were with the Fourth Tennessee Field Artillery."

"That's right," Carhart said.

Kirby was suddenly listening intently.

Reid hesitated as though reluctant to put the next question. "I happen to know that the batteries of the Fourth Tennessee were also in action at the Battle of Shiloh near the landing. Their guns had pinned down a Union outfit that had been cut off from their main line and was trapped in a patch of swampy timber. Am I correct?"

"That's where the most of our batteries was in action," Carhart said. "But I didn't see it. I wasn't there. My section had been stationed along the river to help fight the damned Federal gunboats an' their cussed mortars."

He paused, peering at Reid. "Were you at Shiloh?" he asked.

"The Fourth Tennessee took my arm that day," Reid said. "They wiped out —"

"No!" Norah exclaimed. "Stop it, Reid! It's over! Finished! No, Mr. Carhart, we're not interested."

Kirby spoke harshly. "But, I'm interested, Ben. Your outfit wiped out the infantry regiment I had been serving with — or what was left of it. Slaughtered them in a ditch when they were trying to crawl out of that trap. Can you tell us anything about that?"

"I know about it," Carhart said, disconcerted by the tension around him. "Gunners who worked the cannon told us about it. They wasn't proud of it. Some of 'em looked mighty sick. They said it was like killin' sheep. You fellers didn't have a chance."

"How did they know about that ditch?" Kirby asked.

Carhart again was taken aback by the growing emotion. "I couldn't say," he declared. "I wasn't there."

He added hastily, "I ain't the only man from my outfit that you might be able to get in touch with here in Dakota Territory. Half a dozen other soldiers from the Fo'th came West with me an' are workin' for the railroad at one job or another. Maybe one of them can tell you whatever it is you want to know."

After that nobody said anything for a long time. The wrecking crane retreated down the sidetrack and vanished into the depths of the yards. Evidently nothing had been found to salvage.

Kirby left their hiding place. There was still activity at the scene of the crash, but he remained at a distance, taking refuge in an empty boxcar whose door stood open.

Two of the figures that were silhouetted against the gleam of the torches were those of men who wore braces of six-shooters in holsters. Inchman's fighters, no doubt. He crouched in his hiding place and heard the comments of a few passersby who were leaving the scene. The excitement was subsiding. Antler was returning to its festivities, leaving only railroad workers at the brink of the bluff.

He rejoined the others. "From what I could gather, whatever is left of the parlor car is under thirty feet of water, along with the engines," he said. "Nobody seems to know exactly what happened. Apparently there was no crew aboard the engine. Everybody seems to take it for granted that the parlor car was deserted also."

They waited an exhausting length of time until Kirby decided that they could chance a dash to the sidetracked work train. "Walk on air," he cautioned. "Don't talk. Don't even breathe."

They made it to a weathered coach that stood coupled to two dark baggage cars near the bunting-clad excursion string.

They crept aboard the coach and sat waiting tensely for many minutes, listening. At last they became convinced they had not been seen.

They stretched out on the hard, wooden seats, seeking sleep. Kirby and Reid and Carhart took turns standing watch.

Chapter 13

Vigil was unnecessary. No one came near the coach. Daybreak was pale in the sky when a yard engine puffed down the siding, hooked to their cars and dragged them to the baggage platform at the depot.

The townspeople Norah had recruited were waiting, and came stringing aboard, the women chattering, excited by the prospect of being paid for what promised to be an outing at the expense of the Grand Pacific.

Listening to the talk, Kirby and his companions learned that the wreck of the engine and General Logan's private car was considered an accident.

It was believed the yard engine, somehow, had run wild after the engineer and fireman had alighted for a midnight lunch. The switch to the spur where the palace car was spotted had been left open by some amazing matter of chance, it was believed, diverting the maverick locomotive down the blind siding.

" 'Twas the good Lord whose hand must have thrown the switch," a woman said.

"Sure an' I prayed on me knees that me husband was safe, after I was almost thrown from me bed by the terrible explosion. My prayers were answered by the good Mary. 'Twas me own Brian I was afeared for. But he was safe, brakin' for the shuttle engine up the yards."

"But how can we be sure there was no one kilt, Bridget Murphy," a companion argued. "If any poor divil was caught in the wreck, his body is miles down the river by this time. It will be days before we know if anyone is missin', most likely."

Kirby and his companions were drawing critical glances. Norah and Stella and Timmy had managed to remove some of the traces of their hectic hours, but the three men were obviously unshaven. There was no disguising the lump the bandage formed beneath the shirt on Kirby's arm.

Norah was equal to the occasion. "We look a sight, don't we, Mrs. Murphy?" she gushed. "My brother and I and my friends worked all night, getting things ready and seeing to it they were brought aboard the train. Mr. McCabe injured his arm when something struck him as he worked. It isn't serious."

She smiled. "I hope you ladies and gentlemen can bear with us until we reach the camp and find a chance to freshen up."

Bridget Murphy mellowed and beamed, flattered by being in the limelight. She was a large, kindly woman with the reddened hands of a washwoman. Kirby had a soft place in his heart for Bridget Murphy, for he had known many like her. She was, as she had said, the wife of a brakeman, and she, no doubt, took in washing, ironing, and sewing to keep a comfortable home together.

"Young ladies like you an' Miss Timmy, should not work so hard," she chided. " 'Tis some color you should pinch into your cheeks. Now me daughter, Eileen, spends half her time using such means to beautify herself. 'Tis a vain girl, she is."

Her daughter, Eileen, at her side, was blushing. She was a dewy-eyed colleen of about fifteen, with all the beauty and liveliness of Erin in her pretty face. She needed no pinching for color.

She and Timmy evidently were well acquainted, for they joined company.

"I believe we all should have a little sleep," Kirby said abruptly. "We won't get much rest at Shiloh River."

He had glimpsed two armed men walking down Lincoln Street toward the depot. He recognized them as the pair who

252

had been quarreling at the bar in the Four Aces and who had helped touch off the fake shooting.

His companions understood and stretched out on wooden seats, pretending to try to sleep. This kept their heads below the window line.

Kirby chanced a glance now and then. His pistol was handy in case they came aboard. Reid and Ben Carhart followed his example.

However, the pair remained on the platform. They leaned against the depot wall, thumbs hooked in their gunbelts as they puffed on cigarettes. Their attitudes were of men who felt they were wasting their time.

Kirby decided they were hunters who believed their quarry was already dead.

Presently trainmen began shouting, "All aboard!"

The string of cars lurched into motion. The chatter of the passengers continued. Kirby swung his legs onto a reversed seat and fell into exhausted sleep.

He began dreaming of Shiloh. He kept seeing the twenty-nine fall around him. Fall beneath the blades of the reaper. Blades that always passed over him, leaving him staggering ahead, the ghosts of his comrades at his side.

The bitterness of that day engulfed him. He was beset again by his helplessness, his inability to stop it, the futility of the terrible waste.

A hand was shaking him. He awakened and sat looking into Norah's face. "You were moaning," she said. "You were talking about Shiloh."

"What did I say?" he asked.

"Wild words," she said. "Meaningless." Her eyes were suddenly bright with tears. She turned her head away so that he could not see her emotion. "Will there ever be any peace for you?" she added, her voice choked.

Kirby was silent for a time. "I only wish I was sure," he finally said.

"Sure of what?"

Again Kirby didn't speak for a time. He gazed from the train which was moving across a rolling plain of buffalo grass. The day promised to become blazing hot. Small dust whirlies were already spinning crazily over the dry creek beds.

Far to the south, scattered dark specks broke the pattern of space and hot blue horizons.

"Buffalo!" someone in the car exclaimed.

Heads poked from windows and the passengers talked excitedly. Many of them evidently had never before seen the shaggy beasts of the plains.

Kirby gazed also, but his mind was elsewhere. When he was with the cavalry he had seen the great herds along the Arkansas River. He had watched the northern herd drift across the Dakota plains by the thousands. Always there was fascination and mystery in the spectacle.

In addition, the appearance of the buffalo usually meant something more. The Sioux and Cheyenne followed the herds. It was their source of livelihood. That thought entered his mind now, but it was submerged by the conflict within himself.

Finally he answered Norah. "Your father might be right. Maybe it *was* me that was to blame for what happened to the others that day at Shiloh."

She tried to halt him, but he waved that aside. "I was wounded. Out of my head. I suppose I was babbling crazy things. A Confederate doctor told me not to blame myself for what I'd been saying. Maybe I did tell them about that ditch where the others were slaughtered."

He quit talking for a time. "The next thing I knew I was on a Union steamboat, bound for St. Louis."

Horror was in her eyes. And something else that he wanted from no one, from her least of all. Pity. "Is — is that why you changed so suddenly the day you came to our house at Lockport?" she asked. "Is that why you almost ran when you turned and left?"

"Yes. I had known, of course, that the rest of the regiment had been almost wiped out that day, but I never knew until then that I was blamed for it."

"But you can't blame yourself, even if such a thing really happened."

"*If* it really happened?" There was despair in Kirby. "Then you believe it *did* happen, don't you?"

"I didn't mean it that way."

"There was nobody else who could have told them," Kirby said. "I was the last of the thirty. The only one alive."

"My father will understand that you didn't know what you were saying. He's a kind man, a just man. He's —"

Her voice died. She saw the expression on his face. Irony, disbelief.

"You still hate my father, don't you?" she said slowly.

Kirby had no answer for that. He was thinking of the twenty-nine who had been ordered to their deaths. A kind man! A just man! A man who picked faceless human beings to be slain. Hatred was not the word for what was in Kirby. He wanted justice. He wanted the twenty-nine to sleep in peace, knowing that there was one to speak for them.

She drew away from him. They sat side by side as the train rumbled ahead, but they were now far, far apart.

The engine whistle wailed. Kirby saw the thin brush that marked the course of Shiloh River. They were approaching the steel camp. The big tent that had been set up for entertaining the visitors loomed among the supply sheds and bunk cars.

The train rumbled across the new trestle. The plain, miles to the south, was now clothed in a mottled robe. Buffalo were drifting over the horizon by the hundreds. By the thousands. A major herd.

Norah spoke, breaking the long silence. "What is it? What do you see?"

"Nothing but buffalo," Kirby said.

But he kept gazing to the horizon to the south, hazed now by the thin spume of dust the moving herd was lifting. He believed he had seen the glint of the sun briefly on something far away. A reflection from the horn of some bull buffalo, no doubt. Or perhaps from the metal of a rifle or an ornament worn by an Indian warrior.

The train jostled to a stop and the passengers began filing out of the car. Kirby was the last to arise. Through the window he saw Horace Logan come hurrying to greet his son and daughter as they alighted.

Horace Logan wore his festive garb of white buckskin and the big sombrero. Kirby, through the open window, could hear what was said.

"Everything's ready, dear, thanks to you," Horace Logan said, his arm around his daughter. "Perfect organization, perfect weather. And buffalo hunting right at our door. Did you arrange that also, darling? You're a genius —"

Reid laid a hand on his father's arm. "Norah and I have something to tell you," he said. "It can't wait. It's extremely important. It might take a little time. Where can we go where we can talk without interruption?"

Horace Logan was silenced. Kirby alighted from the car, watching as the Logans walked away and entered the big tent.

Chapter 14

Kirby sat at a late noon meal in the knockdown mess tent. With him were Mike Callahan, Ben Carhart, and two of the crew bosses. Their fare was the substantial food that was served the working force, which had buffalo meat as its bulwark.

They listened to the music of an orchestra from the big tent and to the swelling laughter and hum of conversation where the Easterners were being served food and shellfish brought in at considerable expense by the Grand Pacific. Champagne corks were popping.

Kirby had shaved with a borrowed razor and wore a white cotton shirt that he had borrowed from Mike Callahan. It was midafternoon, for the dude train had not arrived until noon, upsetting the camp routine.

The bunting-clad train had been greeted by the screech of locomotive whistles, the boom of black powder in a small brass cannon, and the roar of pistols fired in the air.

Horace Logan had mounted the bed of a decorated tie wagon to voice the welcoming speech, but his talk had been remarkably brief. Although he had used flowery phrases, he did not seem to actually be in the spirit of the occasion.

His manner, if anything, had been grim. Kirby was sure he knew the reason for this morose mood. Horace Logan had come to the speaking platform directly from his conference with his son and daughter, a conference that had lasted for a long time.

Kirby ate in silence. A weathered, long-haired man in buckskins and moccasins entered the mess tent and said a few words in Callahan's ear.

Callahan abruptly pushed his plate away, his meal unfinished. "Jules don't like the way these buffalo act that are movin' in from the south," he said. "He thinks they're bein' steered in this direction. He smells Indians."

Callahan hurried away, worried, accompanied by the man in buckskins. "Jules is one o' the meat hunters for the camp," one of the crew bosses explained uneasily. "He knows Injuns. He ought to. He's married to a couple of 'em. His two squaws are here in camp. One's Pawnee, the other Crow."

"Where's the damn cal'vry?" Carhart asked.

"Up the line somewhere, chasin' a bunch of braves what stampeded the mules at the gradin' camp yesterday mornin', an' got away with ten, twelve head."

The men looked at each other, the same thought in their mind. "Bait," Carhart said. "An' the cal'vry fell for it."

"I don't reckon a blasted one o' them dudes kin shoot a gun," the crew boss said. "We'd be in a real tight fix if we was jumped by Black Elk an' his whole bunch o' Cheyennes."

"You could be wrong," Carhart said. "There was considerable artillery unloaded from that dude train. A lot of 'em came out here to get themselves a buffalo robe with their own bullet hole in it."

"Shootin' buffalo ain't quite the same thing as facin' up to a full-fledged Cheyenne warrior," the railroad man said. "Not by a long shot. Buffalo don't shoot back."

Kirby took a hand in the conversation. "Don't underestimate these people. Like the rest of us, I've got a hunch that the majority of the men have laid a sight on something other than buffalo — and have been shot at. At places like Gettysburg and Antietam and Shiloh."

A new voice spoke. "And Mr. McCabe should know better than the most of us

261

about who fought and who did not fight at Shiloh. He was there."

Horace Logan had entered the mess tent. The other men, understanding that they were not wanted, hastily excused themselves and left the place. Kirby sat where he was, the tincup of coffee in his hand. He eyed Horace Logan levelly.

"It seems that I owe you a great debt," Horace Logan said, and it was evident he was humbling his pride with an effort. "My son has told me about the scheme to take the railroad away from me. At first I refused to believe it. However, Reid convinced me it is true. I thank you."

He waited, but Kirby did not speak.

"I am doubly indebted to you, apparently," Horace Logan said. "You are the man who interfered on that occasion in Omaha. You may have saved my life by your action at that time. You have now performed an even greater favor. You have averted great financial loss for persons who trusted me and invested in Grand Pacific."

Still Kirby waited in silence. Horace Logan drew a long breath. "I understand your bitterness toward me. It is possible I may have done you an injustice in regard to the disaster at Shiloh. My daughter tells me you were wounded and did not know what you were saying."

"But you really don't believe that, do you?" Kirby asked.

Horace Logan stood stiff and unyielding. He was the military man again, the commander who held the power of life and death over men. "No," he said. "I don't believe that. I do not believe that men say things, even in delirium, that they would not say in their right minds. Brave men. Honorable men."

"If so, then we're birds of a feather," Kirby said. "You sent twenty-nine men to their deaths, hoping to save your own hide from the trap you led the regiment into. There's no question but you were in your right mind at the time. You brand me as a traitor. I brand you as a coward and a murderer. I promised the memory of those twenty-nine men that I'd face you and put that stain where it belongs — on your soul."

Horace Logan stood for moments, and now he was gaunt and gray. But adamant. "Then we have nothing further to discuss, have we, McCabe?" he said hoarsely.

"No," Kirby answered.

Horace Logan wheeled and walked out of the tent, his back ramrod straight, his heels crisply rapping the floor. His son and daughter joined him as he stepped into the sunlight. They had been awaiting the result of his talk with Kirby.

Kirby could see the anxious way they gazed at their father. But, the answer they found in his face palpably was not the one for which they had been hoping.

Some of the life faded out of Norah Logan. And the last of the hope. She turned, gazing at Kirby who still sat at the table in the dimness of the tent. She moved, as though to enter and speak to him. Then she gave it up. She joined her father and walked away.

However, her brother came into the tent and advanced to where Kirby sat. "Nothing's settled, then," he said.

Kirby's silence was the answer. "I'm sorry," Reid said. "You both could be wrong, you know."

When Kirby still did not speak, Reid asked, "What's ahead for you, McCabe?"

Kirby stirred. He ran his fingers tiredly through his hair. "Chile, I suppose. Ray Coleman said he'd have a job for me. There'll be a shuttle train pulling out for Antler before sundown. I'm going to be aboard. I'll catch a boat for Omaha."

"I'm sorry," Reid said again. "More than I can tell you. I was hoping —"

He left it unfinished as though realizing words were useless. He turned to leave.

"What about Inchman?" Kirby asked. "And Martin Garrett?"

"They'll be prosecuted, of course," Reid said. "Along with the group that backed them. My father says he can name them. Unscrupulous bankers and brokers back East."

"Isn't Garrett here? Didn't he come to Shiloh River with the dudes?"

"No. He was supposed to come out on the dude train, but didn't show up. He's still in Antler."

"Or maybe hiding out along with Inchman until sure which way the wind blows," Kirby commented. "They're walking a tightrope and they know it. The charge against them is a lot tougher than framing a swindle. For one thing they're involved in murder. And in attempted murder. They're back of the killing of Lee Venters. And they tried to kill all of us."

"I know," Reid said. "We'll wire Jem Larabee to grab and hold them as soon as we can get a message through to him at Antler."

"As soon as you can get a message through? Isn't the telegraph line — ?"

"Out of order between here and Antler.

Callahan says some bull buffalo probably used a post to scratch off ticks. It's happened before."

Kirby remained at the table for a long time after Reid had left. The place was empty and echoing. The mess boys had cleared the wooden tables and had left.

He presently got to his feet and walked out. Within him was only dullness and a knowledge of a loss that could never be replaced. Norah Logan occupied his thoughts. This was the price Shiloh was exacting after all these years. The realization that he might never see her again left a dread within him.

The vanguard of the great buffalo herd was little more than two miles south of camp. Kirby climbed to the bed of the wagon that had been used as a speaking platform in order to gain a better view. Jules, the meat hunter, joined him.

"I do not like thees," Jules said. "Thees buffalo, they are not acting — what you call eet — natural. They are moving too fast. They are packed too close together."

The buffalo, indeed, were not grazing in the normal manner. They were moving steadily. Walking actually. And, while great herds like this one might appear to be a solid carpet when viewed from a distance,

266

Kirby knew that the animals actually usually traveled in scattered formation, even in small, separate bands.

But this herd was fairly compact. And seemed to be on the prod. Even at this distance, Kirby could see the heads of bulls tossing fretfully. The wind brought their snorting.

The champagne was still flowing in the tent. A team of clog dancers was entertaining on a platform. The steady rhythm of heels and toes was bringing an accompanying tapping of feet from the spectators.

Kirby looked at the sun. He was surprised to see that it was midafternoon. He had not realized the day was passing so swiftly.

"What do you think?" he asked Jules.

The meat hunter wagged his head. "I theenk I will leave thees camp with my women," he said. "I am paid to hunt, not to worry about the scalps of thees fine ones in the tent who fill themselves on wine."

Not long afterward, Kirby saw Jules heading out of camp, kicking his moccasin heels into the ribs of his mount. His wives, on Indian ponies, were belaboring two pack animals, one of which dragged a loaded travois.

Callahan was fuming and frowning, for he had received no word from the crew he had sent out to repair the break in the telegraph line. And the line was still closed. However, he had ordered the shuttle train to be made up, and a switch engine was assembling empty flats and a day coach.

Kirby moved in that direction to board the coach. He turned and gazed at the buffalo herd. They were still coming — steadily.

He suddenly decided he didn't want to leave Shiloh River — at least for the moment.

However, the decision had already been made for him. A man appeared on the east side of the river and came staggering onto the trestle, waving an arm and trying to shout.

Mike Callahan and Kirby were the first to reach him. An arrow was imbedded in his side. His left arm had been broken by a bullet.

"Indians ambushed us about five miles east," the man gasped. "Track torn up, wire down. I'm the only one that got away."

They carried him to a car that served as a hospital and a company doctor began working on him. He was unconscious. He

268

had been one of the crew Callahan had sent out to repair the break in the telegraph line.

Callahan came out of the hospital car, his load of responsibility far deeper. He looked at the oncoming buffalo. "Never saw 'em drift that fast," he said.

Kirby lifted a hand. "What's that? Listen!"

Wild cries were running on the hot afternoon wind. From north of the camp. A rider appeared over a swell, lashing a wild-running Indian pony. It was one of the squaws of Jules, the hunter.

"The Pawnee woman!" Callahan breathed.

Other mounted figures appeared. At that distance they were puppets, unreal, fantastic. Kirby watched the puppets overtake the Pawnee woman. It was over swiftly.

One of the swarm rode clear so that those in the steel camp could see. He was brandishing something in the air. Then they all vanished into the plain, leading away the pony the squaw had been riding.

A speck lay on the plain. The scalped body of the woman.

"Jules has gone under too, most likely," Callahan said hoarsely. "An' the Crow woman. They didn't clear out in time after all."

He looked around. "What were they?" he asked.

"Sioux," a weathered plainsman said. "But there might have been a Cheyenne or two with 'em. I've heerd thet Black Elk an' Brass Kettle have decided to pull together, an' thet they've been exchangin' visits, an' dancin' together."

"If so, there might be a lot of 'em out there," Callahan said. "A couple hundred, maybe."

A man in a fine white suit appeared from the entertainment tent, with a laughing, overdressed woman on his arm. The man had a champagne glass in his hand. He gazed at the buffalo and lifted the glass in a salute.

"Tomorrow, I'll kill me a buffalo and bring the head to you on a silver platter, my dear," he said. "If I can lift it."

Kirby walked into the big tent. The tables were filled. On the platform, an actress, wearing a brilliant red wig and a spangled gown, was singing a gay song and performing a high-kicking dance.

Reid Logan and his father sat at a table with a party of guests. Norah was with them. Kirby beckoned and Reid quickly excused himself and came hurrying.

"Better call off the party," Kirby said. "It

looks like we might be in for trouble. Indians! And maybe more than we can handle."

"Are you sure?"

"No. But all the signs point to it. We're cut off from Antler. Rails torn up, telegraph down. We can't get help from that direction in a hurry. The cavalry has been drawn off to the west. On a wild goose chase, most likely. There are Sioux north of us. They just scalped one of the meat hunter's squaws. The hunter too, probably. It looks like that buffalo herd is being pushed in from the south as a cover for whatever and whoever is back of it."

"The best thing is to tell these people the truth," Reid said.

"Yes. If we're going to be hit, it'll be fast and soon. We've got to get set for whatever comes. Maybe nothing, but it's better to have a gun loaded, just in case."

Reid raced to the platform, halting the entertainer. "Gentlemen! Ladies! There is a possibility that we are in danger of an Indian attack in force. We hope our fears will not be realized, but we must take no chances."

There was a shocked silence. Some of the diners began to wink and look around, suspecting it was a joke.

Kirby joined Reid on the platform. "This is real," he said. "You men see the ladies out of here and to a safer place. Arm yourselves. And make it fast. If it's coming, we haven't much time."

He stood listening to a distant, deep sound of running hoofs. "Stampede!" a man yelled outside the tent. "Buffalo stampede! Comin' right at the camp!"

Another voice, shrill with panic, shouted, "An' Indians comin' in with the buffalo! I kin see 'em! Hundreds of 'em!"

"Move!" Kirby yelled. "Don't panic. You've still got time. But don't waste it."

A rush began from the tent. Kirby and Reid tore aside the canvas walls to permit a faster exit. Emerging into the open, Kirby looked southward. The running buffalo were kicking up a blanket of dust that was rising slowly higher and thickening. Through it he glimpsed mounted figures in the distance, waving blankets. Many riders. Scores.

Women were screaming. The camp was in confusion.

A voice that held the whip-crack of authority spoke. "Silence! You women quit screeching. Get into the sheds or bunk cars and stay there. All you men who brought weapons will arm themselves and stand by for orders. The camp boss will deal out guns from the company armory to all who need them."

The speaker was Horace Logan. He had mounted to a wagon bed. He had abandoned the big white hat, but still wore the gaudy fringed jerkin and breeches. But it was now a uniform. His voice was the voice of a leader. A commander.

The panic faded. Even the more hysterical of the women calmed. They obeyed the order to hurry to shelter. Men raced to find the rifles they had brought with which to hunt buffalo.

Railroadmen had seized the stacked rifles, and other weapons were being dealt out at the supply car by Mike Callahan and assistants. There seemed to be ample ammunition. The majority of the weapons were Sharps muzzleloaders, but there were a number of Henry magazine rifles.

"You, Callahan!" Horace Logan shouted. "Take a squad of men and move out, prepared to split that stampede if it keeps heading toward the camp. You men at the wagon-yards! Hook up two of those tie wagons and rush them out to overturn them so Callahan's men will have some protection and won't be overrun. On the double!"

Kirby doubted if the buffalo posed any real threat to the camp. Buildings and railroad cars offered protection. The odds were that the herd would veer or split of its own accord before it reached the camp. In fact, Kirby saw that the buffalo already were bending slightly westward as though their leaders had scented the presence of civilization and were heading toward the more open plain.

It was the dust the herd was kicking up that offered the real danger. That curtain now cut off all visibility southward. Only the vanguard of the stampede was visible in the fog that rose in the slanting sunlight.

"Mr. Logan!" Horace Logan's voice snapped like a lash, singling out his son. "You will be in command of the line of defense from the mess hall westward to the camp limits."

He paused momentarily. "Mr. McCabe!"

Impelled by his Army training, Kirby stiffened to attention. He met the dominating eyes of the elder Logan.

"Mr. McCabe," Horace Logan said, "you will be in command of the defense line from the mess tent, eastward to the river. I will assign men to your respective areas." This was the military man speaking, the leader.

Kirby saw that Reid also was standing at attention. It seemed the natural thing to do.

The buffalo stampede was still more than a quarter of a mile away. The animals were slowing from their first wild rush. They were settling to a shambling lope, a pace they were capable of maintaining for hours. The slower gait would give the camp more valuable minutes to prepare for the real threat that was coming out of the dust.

Horace Logan was assigning men to the two sections he had devised for defense. "See to it that the barricades are thrown up, Mr. McCabe!" he said. "And you also, Mr. Logan! Topple those wagons. Pile up railroad ties."

Order emerged. Kirby and Reid detailed men to the task of dragging wagons by hand to positions where they were capsized to form barriers. He sent others to bringing crossties from flatcars that stood on a siding.

He found Norah in his path. With her were Stella and Timmy and more than a score of women. Many of them were women from Antler who had come out on the early train to help with the chores, but the majority were visitors. Dudes. They were all pallid, but there was no panic or hysteria among them. The fashionable attire of the visitors ran to bows and ribbons and bustles and puffed sleeves, but they had abandoned their fluttery big hats.

"We can help," Norah said. "Tell us what to do."

The slam of rifle fire began. Mike Callahan's men had opened up on the oncoming buffalo. Another sound became audible, responding to the shooting.

Kirby saw the dread deepen in the faces of Norah and her contingent. Norah spoke again. "We can help. What do you want us to do?"

"If any of you know how to use rifles or pistols, use them," Kirby said. "Get guns at the commissary car."

The sound they had heard was the war cry. These were painted foes who would offer no mercy. They were coming in for the kill.

Chapter 15

The stampede was splitting. A thinning came in the dust. Mounted shadows appeared. Cheyenne warriors, riding low on galloping ponies. Kirby also saw Sioux. Hereditary foes were united in a common cause.

There were hordes of both Sioux and Cheyenne. Hundreds. This was a full-scale attack, Kirby saw. Carefully planned and effectively launched by a brilliant strategist. That must have come from the wise brain of the Sioux, Black Elk.

Men were frantically dealing out rifles and ammunition from the company's supplies. Many women were lining up for arms.

Norah appeared, studying the action of a Henry rifle that had been given her. "Show me how to use this thing," she implored. "I've only fired fowling pieces."

Kirby complied. Timmy and the dewy-eyed Eileen Murphy had been given huge Dragoon pistols. The two girls seemed more frightened of the cumbersome weapons than of the oncoming Indians.

Stella had an Enfield rifle and seemed to know how to handle it. She was showing a bosomy, smartly garbed dowager how to load a similar weapon. She and the dowager apparently had formed an alliance.

Rifles opened up at the west end of the defense line. "Hold your fire!" Reid Logan bellowed. "That's not Indians you're shooting at, you fools. That's Callahan and his men coming in. The next one of you who wastes powder without orders will feel my boot under his shirttail!"

The group that had gone out to split the buffalo herd, came racing back to the barricades. A man, blood flowing from an arrow wound in his arm, staggered to safety back of a wagon where Kirby stood. "Holy Mother!" the man gasped. "The red divils are as thick as the fur on the imp himself."

"Callahan?" Kirby demanded.

"Kilt, pore lad. They was on us before we knew they was that close. The dust. The terrible dust."

But the wind had sprung up, sweeping aside the curtain of dust. The battlefield was clearly revealed. It was sundown, with long shadows racing on the plain. Those shadows were formed by Cheyenne and Sioux fighting men on their war ponies.

They came in, their battle line loosely open. The tails of their ponies were clubbed so as to offer little handhold for a foe. The manes had been cut short for the same reason. The bodies of the riders were greased.

The warriors were also painted with their medicine signs. The faces of the majority wore black. The paint of death, of no quarter. They rode as part of their ponies, hanging offside on surcingle loops, their tough shields of buffalo hides held to guard the breasts of their mounts.

For the most part, they carried rifles. Some were brass-bound muskets, handed down from the trapping days. Other were .50 Springfields. Buffalo guns taken from hunters whose scalps probably hung on the drying boards of the squaws in their villages. A few had the repeating Henrys. All had bows and quivers of the small, deadly war arrows on their backs — a weapon and magazine as deadly as the Henrys at close range. There were hatchets in the belts of their breechclouts. Some had lances.

A powerfully built Cheyenne had the medicine sign of an elk painted on his chest, with a black-dyed feather in his headband. Black Elk himself.

Cheyennes formed the center and left

wing of the Indian line. The entire right wing were Sioux. That would be Brass Kettle and his fighting men.

Kirby shouted, "Fire! Get the ones with the Henrys first! Get the one with the black feather! That's Black Elk!"

Arrows and bullets were already hissing around him. Like Black Elk, he was being singled out as a target by the attackers. He had armed himself with a Henry rifle. He moved among the defenders, firing occasionally. It was all gunfire and powder-smoke now.

The defenders, both men and women, were shooting at the apparitions that came raging toward them. Apparitions that screamed and howled in the frenzy of battle and fired back. Painted riders scorned the fear of death as they came in, lusting to meet, hand-to-hand, these invaders of their land.

Taut-faced men, some in the rough, earth-stained garb of the steel crews, some in linen and broadcloth, screeched and yelled, too, as they fought back. Alongside them stood women whose fine gowns became powder-stained and soiled with the grime of the wagons and the railroad ties. Women with ashen faces and defiant eyes. Men and women who scorned the safety of the barricades, the better to sight their weapons at the wild men of the plains who shouted the savage promise of torture for them.

This was battle! This frenzy. This screaming and shouting and cursing and wild, demonical screeches of satisfaction as hatchets or bullets went home.

The long shadows were at the barricades. Cheyenne and Sioux fought their way inside the camp. Some were on foot, dismounted from slain horses, others were still astride their war ponies as they wielded axes and hurled arrows.

It was all hand-to-hand now. Kirby faced two mounted warriors who were trying to kill him with axes. This was Shiloh again. The Shiloh of Tennessee where the brooks and the muddy tracks of the cannon wheels had run crimson.

He had emptied his rifle. He downed one of his opponents with the last charge in his pistol. He was left defenseless, with the second warrior coming at him, a short-handled ax with a crimson-stained blade poised to brain him.

He evaded the blow, feeling the wicked stir of his hair as the blade grazed him. He had long since lost his hat. He hurled his empty pistol into the face of the Cheyenne.

The impact toppled the Indian, but his foot was held by the loop in the pony's surcingle and the animal carried his slumped body away.

The Cheyenne's ax had fallen to the ground. Kirby snatched it up and walked through the haze of powder-smoke and roar of battle, seeking another foe. Such was the madness of conflict.

But it was over. The Indian attack had failed. The cost was proving too high. Black Elk had mapped out a surprise, but it had gone the other way. The swift organization and fierce strength of the resistance had appalled him. He had seen his warriors decimated. He had seen his fighting men met on equal terms in face-to-face combat.

The presence of the Easterners was a factor he had not anticipated. It had evened the numbers. Their fighting spirit had decided the battle.

Black Elk bitterly gave the signal to withdraw. Brass Kettle, the Sioux chief, was dead, and his warriors were already losing heart. The camp was suddenly clear of Indians, with only the rattle of hoofs of the retreating war ponies in the ears of the defenders.

Kirby looked around dazedly. Stella

Venters was kneeling beside the body of the bosomy dowager. Stella was praying, for the dowager was dead, an arrow in her breast.

The bodies of wounded and the slain lay at the barricades. A woman began screaming frenziedly.

"Eileen! Merciful Mother of God, protect her! The red divils have taken her! My little Eileen! Stop them! Stop them!"

The voice was that of Bridget Murphy, who, along with her daughter, had been among those hired to wait table for the visitors.

Half a dozen mounted Indians were riding north, a long rifleshot distant. They were young braves. Sioux. One had a captive on his pony.

The prisoner was the fifteen-year-old Eileen Murphy, she of the shy eyes and rosebud beauty. The braves evidently had crept in by way of the river brush during the battle and seized the girl, escaping unseen out of camp.

Bridget Murphy raced frantically on foot out of camp in a mother's hysterical attempt to follow her child.

Men overtook her and carried her back to safety. She fought them and screamed that they were cowards.

"My poor, poor baby!" she sobbed. "Let me go. I do not want to live!"

Horace Logan lay on a blanket, with his daughter working over him. Norah apparently had escaped injury, but her father had been felled by a war club and was unconscious. He had also been struck in the leg by an arrow.

A sudden silence came, broken only by Bridget Murphy's sobbing. Every face was turned in one direction. Toward Kirby.

They were awaiting orders. The majority of them had seen service in one army or the other. As the one of senior military rank, they considered him in command now. Reid Logan stood waiting also.

The decision was his and his alone. He stood burdened suddenly by a terrible responsibility. Horrified by it.

To the north, the braves were vanishing into the depths of the plains with their captive. His mind assayed the situation. The raiding party would almost certainly circle south eventually to join the main band of Indians. If the girl was ever to be recovered, it would have to be done before darkness closed in. The time was short.

He accepted the duty. He knew there could be no appeal from his decision. Right or wrong, the responsibility was his.

"All right," he said. "We've got to get that girl back." He debated it a moment, then added, "I'll take six of you with me. We can't weaken the defense here any more than that. Seven of us should be enough to do the job."

He lifted his voice. "Any of you wranglers who are still on your feet, get to the corrals and rig seven horses. Fast! See to it that they're the best animals in the string!"

He leaped to the top of a barricade and looked down at the men. The silence deepened, became almost an electric force. He could see the blood receding from faces as they realized what this meant. The fear was there, the mental battle against flinching. For they knew that the odds were that any man who was singled out to ride with him would never return.

For an instant Kirby could not force himself to speak. But it must be done. He lifted a hand, pointed a finger. "You there in the riding britches and fancy coat. You look like a fox hunter. Are you married? No? Very good. I'll take you, for one. You'll find this a little more exciting than riding to hounds."

He singled out another. "And you there with the sideburns and black mustache. You fought real good. I saw you at the barricades. You're a string bean and wiry. You look like you know a horse has four legs. Right? You'll do."

Both of the two he had selected were Easterners and evidently well-to-do by their garb. The blood receded entirely from their faces, leaving their eyes dark and flat. But they moved forward without a word of protest and stood below Kirby.

Four more, Kirby thought, and there was an agony of protest in him that he must go on with this. He picked one of the crew bosses, who was young and sinewy and a weathered, hawk-eyed man in a hunting shirt and old army trousers whom he surmised was one of the meat hunters for the camp. The fifth man was a stalwart, red-headed Irishman from the steel gang.

He hesitated again, gazing at the frozen, colorless faces, seeing the fight to avoid showing the white feather. He looked down at Reid Logan. There was desperate appeal in Reid's eyes. He wanted to be chosen. But a man with one arm . . .

A hoarse voice spoke. "You, Mr. Logan, will join the detail."

The speaker was Horace Logan. He had revived and was sitting up, pushing his daughter aside. He had resumed command, and his first order was to send his own flesh and blood to possible death.

Reid drew a long breath. "Thank you, sir!" he said.

Kirby spoke. "That's all! Come on, men! Fast!"

He led the way at a run to where hostlers were straining at the cinches on animals that had been roped out.

Kirby made a hasty appraisal of arms and saw to it that every man had a loaded pistol and rifle. The plainsman carried a belt hatchet. Kirby also armed himself with a hatchet. It was an Indian weapon that had been taken from a dead Sioux.

"Mount!" he said.

They rode at a gallop out of camp. Looking back, he saw Norah shading her eyes against the slant of the sun. When he looked back before the swells shut out sight of the camp, she was still standing, watching.

The sun sank below the horizon. White clouds became golden ships floating in an azure sky. The great herd of buffalo had vanished and only a few scattered animals were visible in the distance. The young Sioux had been swallowed by the vastness of the purple land to the north.

Far to the south, the main body of the defeated Indians came into sight for a time, crossing higher ground. Tiny figures at that distance, they faded into the shadows of the oncoming twilight and the land was now empty. Empty of all but the seven who rode boot-to-boot.

"They won't be in any hurry to harm the gal," the plainsman said. "They'll want to wait a time when some of our people will know about it. See it, maybe. Or hear it."

He was talking about torture. And about young, pretty Eileen Murphy.

"Who is this girl?" the man in the fox-hunting coat asked. "Who was the woman who screamed? Was that her mother?"

"Yes," Kirby said. "Her mother. A washwoman."

"There'll be more'n the handful of braves we saw ridin' away with the gal," the plainsman said. "There's bound to have been more of 'em waitin' out there to ambush anybody what came high-tailin' to follow 'em."

Kirby nodded. "Our only chance is to hit them after they think they're in the clear. They're surely going to circle south and join the main bunch. My guess is that they'll turn west, then south. But they could swing east. What's your guess? And what is your name?"

"Yancey. Bill Yancey. One guess is as

good as another. An' one guess is all we're goin' to git if she's to have any chance at all. We've got to hit 'em fast, hope to grab her an' whiz out o' the hornet's nest with enough of us left to get her back to camp."

All except Reid Logan were uneasily, covertly glancing at each other. Each man was wondering if the same question was in the minds of his companions.

Kirby was thinking of the day at Shiloh when he had been asking himself that same question.

"Why me? Why was I picked to advance into the face of death? There were so many others . . ."

These men were brave. They were not flinching or protesting, no matter what their inner thoughts. But in all of them was the full desire to live.

Kirby spoke abruptly to the man in the fox-hunting garb. His voice was rough, almost brutal. "You may be killed, trying to save the daughter of a washwoman. Do you understand that?"

"Why yes," the man said. "And so might you, my friend."

"What is your name?" Kirby asked.

The man smiled tightly. "Smedley Arlington Trenton. Smed Trenton to my friends. Incidentally, I was a sharpshooter with the 1st Massachusetts Dragoons. Served nearly four years."

They rode on. Kirby was thinking that if he had guessed wrong and they failed to intercept their quarry before dark there would be nothing to do but turn back. However, at this latitude at this time of year, twilight lingered on the purple land.

Ahead of them, a jackrabbit bounded over the crest of a swell, looming startlingly large against the darkening sky. Another rabbit appeared, fleeing northward.

Kirby raised a hand and they pulled up the horses. They could now hear the grunting, hoarse complaining of prairie dogs beyond the swell.

"They're over that rise," Kirby said. "Breathe deep and long. Fill your lungs. Our only chance, as Yancey said, is to hit them fast and hard, then run. Don't give them time to kill the girl. Logan and myself will try for the girl. We'll go in, shooting. But keep bullets away from her. If we fail, turn back and try to make it to camp. You'll be on your own. God bless you. I'll see you somewhere again. And buy you a drink. A drink of ambrosia and nectar, maybe. But a drink."

Without raising his voice, he said, "Charge!"

They hurled the horses into motion and swept over the rise side-by-side. Directly ahead were more than a score of young Sioux on tired ponies. The odds had mounted to more than three to one.

One of the braves carried Eileen Murphy on his pony. They had stripped most of the clothing from her and were jeering and jabbing her with sticks, but she was, at least, still alive.

The Sioux had believed they were safe from pursuit. They froze for an instant, staring at the riders who came charging over the skyline.

Three or four of them died in the first rifle volley. Riderless ponies reared and added to the confusion. The Indians snatched out rifles and pulled triggers. Many of the weapons failed to explode. Faulty priming or failure to reload.

Then the seven were among them and it was hand-to-hand. Kirby emptied his rifle and used his six-shooter. Around him the others were firing pistols. He reached the side of the Sioux who was trying to use Eileen Murphy as a shield.

Smedley Arlington Trenton killed the Sioux with a shot from his pistol. A moment later a war ax was buried in Trenton's head and he toppled from the saddle.

Kirby dragged the girl astride the neck of his horse, clamping an arm around her, shielding her with his own body.

He looked down at Smedley Trenton, whose body lay beneath the churning hoofs of rearing horses.

"I sent you into this," he said. "I'll never forget you."

Reid was at his side. They fought their way clear, with the girl limp and fainting in Kirby's grasp.

One other of the five who had gone in with them, emerged from the dust and confusion. He was the plainsman, Bill Yancey. And he went down in the next instant, pierced by an arrow.

Kirby and Reid Logan crouched in the saddles, lashing their horses to greater effort. Reid's shirt hung in shreds. There was a crimson slash across his chest, the mark of a knife or an arrow. Like Kirby, he was looking back, hoping, praying that some of the others would ride clear.

But none of the others appeared.

Arrows followed them. Reid's horse was hit, but the injury seemed to he minor and only goaded the animal to greater speed. A faint-hearted pursuit began, but was quickly given up by the Sioux on their tired ponies.

Eileen Murphy began to sob hysterically. "You're safe now," Reid told her.

"Those other men," she wept. "Those other poor, poor men back there."

Kirby and Reid let their winded horses slow to a walk until the animals recuperated. They reloaded their six-shooters.

Stars were blazing in the sky when the lights of the steel camp appeared ahead. Kirby lifted a shout and men came racing to meet them.

They were surrounded by a cheering crowd as they rode into camp. The cheering had started when Eileen Murphy was sighted, but the sound lost volume and faded into dead silence when it was realized that only two of the seven were returning.

They slid exhaustedly to the ground. The girl ran to the arms of her mother. Norah stood, helping support her father, who leaned on improvised crutches. Timmy Venters came rushing to Reid and threw her arms around him, babbling wild words.

Horace Logan's haggard eyes asked a question of Kirby. "The others didn't make it," Kirby said. "They covered me when I rode out with the girl. That's why we're alive."

"I've got something to say to you, McCabe," Horace Logan began. "Something that I've learned from —"

A train whistle sounded in the night. A headlight appeared beyond the bridge. "It's from Antler," a man shouted. "It looks like it's filled with men. Reinforcements, in case the Indians come back. Maybe they're bringing doctors an' supplies."

The crowd streamed to meet the incoming train. It consisted of two day coaches and several baggage cars. The coaches were filled with men and bristled with guns.

A man wearing a conductor's cap leaped from the cab of the engine. "Thank the Lord!" he exclaimed. "We heard that you was all dead. Massacred by Indians. We —"

A babble of questions drowned him out. Horace Logan, supported by his son, pushed to the front and shouted for silence. "How did you find out we'd been under attack?" he asked. "The telegraph line is still out."

"One of the repair crew that was sent out from here to fix the line hid in the bush when the Indians jumped them. Later on, he managed to get a message east to Antler. He said he could hear a terrible lot of shooting from the direction of the steel camp, but that it had ended. He said you'd all been killed. We got up a special train and come through, hell for leather. We didn't bother stopping to fix the telegraph. About half a mile of it was cut."

The man quit talking, realizing that the attention of Horace Logan and his son had shifted.

Kirby suddenly moved forward. The citizens of Antler who had come on the relief train were flooding from the cars. Three men, who were among them, halted the moment their feet reached the platform. One was Martin Garrett. With him was Barney Inchman. At Inchman's shoulder was his gunman, Parson Slate.

The oil lamps in the coaches laid a pattern of flickering light on the faces of the trio. Martin Garrett's expression was that of sheer despair. Barney Inchman's heavy features had frozen into a mask of fury. He was a man who had suddenly found himself in a corner from which the only escape was by violence or death. He was in no mood to surrender. Parson Slate's bony face bore no expression at all.

They were seeing ghosts. They had joined the relief train in the belief that Horace Logan was dead, slain in the supposed massacre, and there was now nothing in their way toward eventually taking over control of the Grand Pacific.

Kirby pushed past Horace Logan and moved apart from him. He found Reid at his side.

Martin Garrett uttered a strangled sound and lifted both hands in the air. "No!" he said hoarsely.

"You thief!" Horace Logan said. "You traitor!"

"I'm not armed!" Garrett said desperately.

But Barney Inchman was armed. And so was Parson Slate. Inchman was seeing the total ruin of the elaborate fraud he had spent months and years in perfecting. His future was prison at best, and perhaps the gallows. He shifted his body slightly in a position to go for the six-shooter he had in a holster strapped beneath his unbuttoned linen jacket.

Parson Slate faced the issue with dead eyes that measured his opponents with no thought other than that he was the faster and would kill them both. His right arm had proved its speed and its power to launch the lightning in the past. He was sure of his ability.

Kirby was looking at Parson Slate. "You

murdered Lee Venters, didn't you Slate," he said. And that statement — for it was a statement and not a question — made the issue clear between them.

Slate did not answer. Martin Garrett shrank away from his companions. Bystanders became aware of what was developing. A stampede began to escape from the line of fire.

Kirby knew that he would live or die in the next moment. He knew the chances were that he would be slower than the gunman and that he might fall there on this dimly lighted platform.

"Take Inchman," he said to Reid Logan.

Then Slate was drawing. Kirby also drew. He flipped the hammer of his six-shooter and released it in one sweeping, gusting desire to stay alive.

He felt the hard, grinding smash of a bullet tearing into his flesh. The blow was felling him. As he reeled, he had a vision of Parson Slate falling also, and of the smoking pistol dribbling from Slate's grasp.

He heard the slam of Reid Logan's six-shooter at his side, and knew that Inchman was also shooting. He saw Inchman's body jerk to the hammerblow of a bullet.

Then the blackness closed in.

★ ★ ★

It was long afterward when the blackness faded. He lay in a railroad car on a train that was moving. Daylight had come. The morning sun was shining brightly.

Norah was at his side. "Don't die, McCabe!" she implored. "You've got to live! I won't let you die!"

She kissed him. Her lips were tender and so very warm and soft.

"So this is heaven," he croaked.

She kissed him again, then wept. "You *are* better," she choked. "You *are* going to live."

"Forever," he said. "If you will just stay right there."

Her father loomed above her, leaning on his improvised crutches. "We're on our way back to Antler where all you people can be better taken care of," he said. "But, for you and I, McCabe, we are going back much farther than that. Back to Shiloh. There's much to be done. And undone."

Kirby raised his head. The car was lined with wounded on pallets. Ben Carhart lay nearby. He evidently had been badly injured, but he managed to grin and wink at Kirby. "Nice seein' you back with us, Cap'n," he said.

Stella and Timmy were present. Along

298

with other women they were helping care for the patients. Reid stood back of his father, smiling.

"Slate?" Kirby asked. "Inchman?"

Horace Logan answered. "Slate is dead. He died instantly. Inchman will live. Live to hang, perhaps. Along with Garrett. Reid escaped injury in the fight."

Kirby was silent for a time. "I was wrong," he finally said. "Wrong about Shiloh. You had to send us in that charge that day. Just as I had to pick the men to die to save that girl. The other twenty-nine know that. They know everything now."

"And so do the men who rode with you yesterday," Horace Logan said gently. "If you were wrong about me, the wrong I did you was so vastly greater there is nothing I can do except say, forgive me."

It was Norah who answered the unspoken question in Kirby's eyes. "Yes. We found men in the work crews who had served the Confederate cannon that day at Shiloh, just as Ben Carhart said."

Her father nodded. "We talked to two of them. That was what I started to tell you last night. The presence of that ditch was known to their officers all day long. Their captain had been waiting for us to try to use it as a way of escape. One of their artillerymen even owned the little farm on which we were fighting. He had scraped out that ditch himself a few seasons earlier to drain his cotton patch."

General Logan's voice was filled with emotion. "Nobody talked. No Union soldier. The only one I accused of talking remained true to his oath, true to his faith. I'll see to it, Kirby McCabe, that this stain is removed from you. Back home, everywhere. It was the war. The accursed war. Like those brave men who went out with you yesterday and never came back."

Reid spoke. "I'm afraid you're not going to see South America, McCabe. Not for the present at least. We have a job for you. Someone has to replace Martin Garrett. The Grand Pacific is going to be built. In fact we were given a vote of confidence this morning by our visiting friends, and they pledged to subscribe to a pleasing amount of stock. We had told them the truth about the situation."

Kirby felt Norah's fingers tighten on his hand. "That isn't the only reason you're not going to South America," she said.

Kirby kept looking up at her. Along with the mourning for the brave, there was, for the first time in years, peace in his own heart.

We hope you have enjoyed this Large Print book. Other Thorndike, Wheeler or Chivers Press Large Print books are available at your library or directly from the publishers.

For more information about current and up-coming titles, please call or write, without obligation, to:

Publisher
Thorndike Press
295 Kennedy Memorial Drive
Waterville, ME   04901
Tel. (800) 223-1244

Or visit our Web site at:
www.gale.com/thorndike
www.gale.com/wheeler

OR

Chivers Large Print
published by BBC Audiobooks Ltd
St James House, The Square
Lower Bristol Road
Bath BA2 3SB
England
Tel. +44(0) 800 136919
email: bbcaudiobooks@bbc.co.uk
www.bbcaudiobooks.co.uk

All our Large Print titles are designed for easy reading, and all our books are made to last.

Cross-Fire